From ... *n Crime*

There was a chorus of protest from the assembled garden owners. Nobody has such a keen sense of property as the person who grows it himself. They all began to talk about depredations made on their own gardens: wall-trained trees broken down by people climbing over, and apples and pears stolen weeks before they would be ripe. Now, vegetables were being taken too. Everybody agreed that it was getting worse since the war.

"It used to be only boys out for a lark," said Mr. Nichol-Jervis, "but now it's organized crime."

Linnaeus Bex could not resist adding,

"Common or garden crime."

"But they won't get away with it here," Mr. Nichol-Jervis went on. "Look!" He pointed to an angle of the wall where a tree on the far side provided an easy way of climbing over. The top of the wall was all sticky and glistening with a recent coat of tar.

"They'll spoil their clothes on that," said Mr. Nichol-Jervis with satisfaction, "and we'll have a clue to identity, if the Guards get a move on."

The tar was easily the most popular exhibit of the garden tour. Everybody hailed the idea as brilliant, and those who had also suffered from garden thefts determined to copy it. Things looked bad for local lawbreakers, with even old Miss Milfoyle breathing venom and hoping the Guards would catch somebody and make an example of them.

"Bikh would be too good for them," laughed Lord Barna. "By the way, Wendy, you never showed it to me."

"Why, there it is." Wendy pointed to a nearby clump of dark blue-flowered spikes. The *Aconitum ferox* is lower growing than the best garden monkshoods, and not at all impressive. They all looked at it respectfully.

"Want some?" Wendy asked the Earl.

"No thanks," he smiled, "I have no murderous intentions."

"Well, if you develop any, you know where to come."

Books by Sheila Pim

Crime Fiction

Common or Garden Crime (1945)
Creeping Venom (1946)
A Brush with Death (1950)
A Hive of Suspects (1952)

Novels of Irish life

The Flowering Shamrock (1949)
Other People's Business (1957)
The Sheltered Garden (1965)

Non-Fiction

Getting Better (1943)
Bringing the Garden Indoors (1949)
The Wood and the Trees (1966, 1984)

Common or Garden Crime

an Irish gardening mystery by
Sheila Pim

The Rue Morgue Press
Boulder, Colorado

Common or Garden Crime
Copyright © 1945
Copyright © 2001
ISBN: 0-915230-36-4

FIRST AMERICAN EDITION

The Rue Morgue Press
P. O. Box 4119
Boulder, Colorado 80306

Printed by Johnson Printing
Boulder, Colorado

Introduction
The Many Gardens of Sheila Pim

SHEILA PIM wrote her first detective novel, *Common or Garden Crime*, to satisfy her father's thirst for detective stories, the publication of which had been curtailed thanks to the paper shortages which affected neutral Ireland during the "Emergency"—or World War II, as it was called in most other parts of the globe. The book turned into something of a collaboration, at least when it came to research, with Sheila and her accountant father pooling their knowledge of gardening and sharing details about the habits of their Dublin neighbors.

Such attention to detail is important, since the puzzle is very much secondary to character and place in Pim's detective novels. Her amateur sleuths are not the usual meddlesome busybodies or smug dilettantes so common to the period, but generally sensible women who go to the police only when they think they have good reason to do so and who would never dream of interfering with the progress of a criminal investigation. When Inspector Lancey remarks to Ivor that his Aunt Lucy is in a minority in Ireland in her respect for law and order, he matter-of-factly explains, "Oh, we're very Anglo." Lancey knows exactly what he means. After all, Ireland is a country, as Pim points out, in which doing jail time is not considered a disgrace given the number of prominent citizens who have been incarcerated from time to time for political reasons. It's no wonder, Pim observes, that Ireland leads the world in prison reform.

Pim's detective novels are unique for the period in other aspects as well. They follow an unusual format by presenting two non-adversarial parallel investigations. While the Guard—Ireland's version of Scotland Yard—pursues the killer using tried and true police routine, Pim's amateur sleuth, privy to many of her neighbors' secrets, quietly conducts her own inquiries, usually arriving at the same conclusion as the police, whom she generally presents in a favorable light.

Although representatives of the Civic Guards appear in all four of Pim's detective novels, it would be a mistake to label this quartet a conventional series or even to call them police procedurals. Each is a standalone detective novel meant to be read independently. Lancey and his crew, with a few modest exceptions, are ciphers shown only in the exercise of their professional duties.

Pim's books might better be described as novels of manners in which the lives of perfectly ordinary people are disrupted by an extraordinary event—murder. Oddly enough, however much Sheila's father relished his thrillers, Pim was one of the first novelists in a country famous for its storytellers to attain any degree of fame as a mystery writer, and only the last of her four mysteries, *A Hive of Suspects*, was published in the United States. *Common or Garden Crime* appeared in 1945, followed a year later by *Creeping Venom* (the only book in which the amateur sleuth is solely responsible for solving the mystery), *A Brush with Death* (1950) and *A Hive of Suspects* (1952). Pim's relatively short career as a mystery writer ended a year before her countrywoman Eilis Dillon, primarily a children's book author, published the first of her three highly praised but also relatively obscure mysteries, all of which were eventually published in the U.S.

Why neither Dillon nor Pim was able to obtain the same degree of commercial success in America that was enjoyed by many of their sisters in crime across the Irish Sea in England is difficult to explain, unless you subscribe to the conventional wisdom that American readers are interested only in mysteries set at home or in England. St. Patrick's Day aside, most Americans know as much about Irish life and society as they do about conditions in Canada. Whereas most Americans recognize the name Scotland Yard, only a few could identify the Guard as its Irish counterpart. Even today only a handful of Irish mysteries appear on the U.S. market, and the most successful of these, the Inspector McGarr series by Bartholomew Gill, is written by an American of Irish descent.

Anglo or not, it is the Irishness of Pim's books, such as her portrait of day-to-day village life during World War II in *Common or Garden Crime*, that gives them their special flavor. Contemporary critics greeted her mysteries with enthusiasm. "Do some more, Miss Pim," pleaded the *Sphere*, describing her books as having "excellent characterization, considerable humour and a nice appreciation of what is thrilling in a murder mystery and what is not." Our favorite review, from the *Observer*, called her mysteries "Vivacious as a wall lizard." We're not altogether sure what the writer meant but we've certainly never run across another detective novel described in such terms. But it was The *Times Literary Supplement* that best singled out those qualities that put Pim in a class all her own when it praised her second book for the same "humour and shrewd observation of small town Irish life" as was found in her first effort. These mysteries of manners as well as her mainstream novels of modern Irish life led critics to proclaim her the Angela Thirkell of Ireland, and there is a good bit of Trollope as well as Austen in her perceptive portraits of a particular time and place in her native land.

Pim was one of the first mystery writers to fully integrate a gardening background into her novels. Not only are horticultural details pivotal to the plots but they govern the characters' daily lives. For Pim, as well as her protagonists, gardening was not just a hobby but a necessary (and rewarding) way of life. The bounty of the kitchen garden was a constant source of fruits and vegetables for the table, especially welcome during the lean years of the Emergency, and the flower garden was not only esthetically pleasing but was the basis for such social diversions as the flower show held at the Bexes in *Common or Garden Crime*. Like most of her friends and neighbors, Lucy Bex knows the Latin names for all the plants in her garden, appreciates the value of a nicely composting manure heap and is familiar with the best ways of putting food by for the winter. Throughout the story she is nearly as preoccupied with bottling her tomato harvest as she is with uncovering the murderer.

There appears to be a great deal of the author's own character in her heroines, especially Lucy Bex. Like Lucy, who keeps house for her widowed brother Linnaeus and helped raise her nephew Ivor, Sheila Pim never married and had to make any number of professional sacrifices to make a pleasant home for her father Frank, a widower, and her developmentally disabled two-year-older brother Tom. In spite of these hardships, Pim evidently enjoyed the same kind of loving family atmosphere that permeates the Bex household.

It's a little harder to reconcile Pim, the birthright Quaker, with the Lucy who applauds the eventual execution of the murderer and supports Ivor's decision to join the Royal Air Force. But those were different as well as difficult times, and the Bex family seemed to march to a different drummer than their neighbors in many other aspects. Much of the appeal of *Common or Garden Crime* lies in its portrait of life in Ireland, only a few years free of English rule, during World War II. The Protestants and

Catholics of Clonmeen mix with only a few problems, so long as they confine themselves to garden talk and are of the same social class, but Anglo families like the Bexes have cast their lot with England while their Catholic counterparts cannot forget the oppression suffered at the hands of the English Parliament.

Pim herself was born in Dublin on September 21, 1909, of a Quaker father and an English mother. Her twin brother Andrew survived only two weeks. Her older brother, Tom, two years her senior, was born developmentally disabled—possibly autistic—and would need constant care throughout his 57 years. Sheila was educated at the French School in Bray, County Wicklow, and "finished" at La Casita in Lausanne, Switzerland, where she perfected her French. In 1928, she went to Girton College, Cambridge, where she took a Tripos in French and Italian. This was apparently one of the happiest periods of her life, according to her friends at the Historical Society of the Religious Order of Friends. This euphoria is reflected in an oil painting done of her at the time, showing her as "a long slim figure with long brown hair down her back, dressed in a pretty summer frock, and a little smile showing her sense of humour."

But the good times were soon to end. Shortly before finals, Margaret Pim took ill and Sheila returned to Dublin to look after her mother and provide some diversion for Tom. During this period, she worked for a short time as a typist for the Dublin Royal Society. When her mother died in 1940, Sheila was forced to abandon many of her own projects, including botanical studies, to run her father's household. This situation was further complicated when Sheila herself took ill and underwent a long recuperation, which led to her first book, a slender volume called *Getting Better: A Handbook for Convalescents*, published in 1943, while she and her family were living in Campfield, Dundrum, Dublin. This is the same locale and year in which *Common or Garden Crime* is set and indeed there are sections in which she offers advice on how to handle shortages during the Emergency.

The Pim family lived in a large Georgian house replete with a large walled garden much like that of the Bexes, where they grew fruits and vegetables and where Sheila began to develop her knowledge of horticulture, which eventually led to her column "Gardening Notes" for the *Irish Times*. She also contributed to a specialty magazine, *My Garden*, for a number of years. Her first unsolicited submission differed from other manuscripts submitted to the magazine, according to editor Theodore A. Stephens, as it was "on rather better paper than usual, typed very expertly and had obviously been written specially for *My Garden* and not just for any gardening paper. An accompanying note asked for the favour of consideration and, if approved, suggested a fee (very modest) which would be acceptable to the writer." It's a note that one can well imagine Lucy Bex or Hester Fennelly of *A Brush with Death* writing. Many of those essays were eventually collected in *Bringing the Garden Indoors* (1949), a slender volume that offered advice on how to extend and enjoy the fruits of the garden throughout the year.

She was fond of reading the *Boys Own* papers of the nineteenth century which she found "packed with curious information of a practical sort." Another hobby was the collection of slang, clichés, and amusing habits which she found in thrillers and in popular American magazines. Some of this material was used to entertain Tom, who continued to need constant diversion.

When her father died in 1958, Sheila moved with Tom to Old Conna, Bray, where they were forced to make do without resident domestic help. About this time Sheila once again was hit by a major illness. As a result, she encouraged Tom to be a bit more independent and, for the first time in his life, he learned to travel about town on his own and to use the public library. Sheila herself volunteered to run what passed for a museum at the Friends Historical Society.

During this period, she published her last mainstream novel, *The Sheltered Garden* (1965), a witty novel of manners with a few mystery elements but a great deal of gardening. She was also busy researching her most famous work, *The Wood and The Trees*, a biography of Augustine Henry, an Irish doctor who became one of the foremost plant collectors of his age and co-wrote the definitive book on the trees of Great Britain and Ireland. It was published in 1966 and revised and reissued in 1984.

In 1964, Tom was killed in an accident and Sheila became free for the first time in her life to pursue her own interests full-time, but oddly enough these did not include writing fiction. Instead, she threw herself into her work at the Friends Historical Society, researching and conserving archival embroideries and portraits. She also began what was to be a lifelong commitment to improving the lot of the Irish Travellers. Ostracized by much of Irish society, the Travellers are a nomadic people native to Ireland who follow a gypsy-like life and speak their own language, Shelta, which is closer to English than to Gaelic. Travellers are sometimes known as Tinkers—now considered a derogatory term—partly because many of them worked as tinsmiths, as well as itinerant farm laborers and door-to-door salesmen. Today there are some 24,000 Travellers in the Republic of Ireland, 1,500 in Northern Ireland, 15,000 in England and 7,000 in the United States. In addition to their traditional occupations, many modern Travellers are involved in scrap and antiques dealing.

In the mid-1960s, just as the civil rights movement was erupting in the United States, many Irish began to protest the discriminatory treatment afforded Travellers, who were resisting attempts to force them to abandon their traditional life-styles and be assimilated into the general Irish population. Pim became active in the Travellers' civil rights movement, taking many Traveller children into her home and eventually adopting an entire family which had been abandoned to the care of their travelling grandfather. She studied Traveller culture and shared her knowledge of their life-style with as many people as possible as she watched her adopted family grow, prosper and marry.

In Sheila Pim's last years, her growing deafness forced her to move into a sheltered housing complex where she still managed to grow a few herbs by her door. She fell ill and died on December 16, 1995, at the age of 86. In writing about Augustine Henry, Pim noted that even though he was neither empire-builder nor gunman nor agitator, he still put together a remarkable life. The same could be said for Sheila Pim. In a life filled with adversity she still reaped a bountiful harvest, as a dutiful daughter, a caring sister, an expert gardener, an advocate for social justice and surely the most accomplished writer of Irish detective fiction of her age. The lines from George Herbert that she quoted to describe Henry would serve equally well as her own epitaph:

"Only the sweet and virtuous soul
like seasoned timber, never gives."

Tom & Enid Schantz
January 2001
Boulder, Colorado

Common or Garden Crime

Gardening tips from Sheila Pim's
Bringing the Garden Indoors

January

Our first rows of Peas and Broad Beans are already out in the ground under cloches, sown since November. Both crops came in early in May last year, but the Peas were scanty, having suffered mass attacks of snails. When sowing them one should prepare the trench and have the cloches over it for a week or two before putting down the seeds. Lettuce, sown under cloches before the winter, came in last March. Growing it this way one should not manure the grounds or the plants will bolt.

In ordering French Beans I demand a genuinely stringless variety. Another item is Sugar Peas, as prolific as they are delicious, and very pretty as a flowering hedge too.

At the end of the list I put down Garlic, and there are immediate protests that we don't want that in the garden. But I only mean to lay in a small store for cooking. All my attempts to obtain it from greengrocers have hitherto failed, and now that I see it down on a seedsman's list I will have a quarter of a pound. The general opinion is that this ought to be more than enough to supply our requirements for a year.

All one need ever do with Garlic is to rub it on the bowl. I have one recipe for a soup which begins "Crush a clove of garlic in the bottom of the bowl. . ." and ends ". . .remove the garlic." This is beyond me.

CHAPTER I
Everything in the Garden Is Lovely

VARIOUS AUTHORITIES have spoken highly of gardening as an occupation. Bacon calls it "the purest of human pleasures," and Voltaire recommends people to cultivate their gardens instead of worrying about the war.

Most of the inhabitants of Clonmeen took Voltaire's advice. Clonmeen is a village on the hem of the outskirts of Dublin, not yet counted as a suburb by the Local Government authorities, and certainly not by the inhabitants. Most of these live in roomy, old-fashioned houses with large gardens, where the basement is a problem (owing to the fuel shortage) but the vegetables are a great standby. There is always plenty to do, planting, propagating, pruning, pickling and preserving, and coping with seasonal gluts of country produce. As this takes up a good deal of time, and it is hard to get about with no cars, the place is quiet, not to say dull. But not too quiet for crime. We are also told that evil began in a garden.

Beechfield is the Nichol-Jervises' place, and one of the grander houses of Clonmeen, with a fine beech avenue and considerable grounds. To cross these by way of the front and back avenue is a pleasanter walk, for those privileged to use it, than going round outside the high boundary wall and saves about a quarter of a mile.

The Bexes live at Annalee Lodge, a nice pink house with a half-acre garden and a paddock, enclosed in a triangle of roads with Annalee House and Annalee Hall. These are Victorian villas with three or four acres apiece; all the Annalees had been divided up from an earlier farm holding which was all one. Annalee House belongs to the McGoldricks, old and respected inhabitants like the Bexes and the Nichol-Jervises. Annalee Hall had been taken, a few months before the story opens, by the

Osmunds, about whom local opinion was still making up its mind.

One morning in the summer of 1943, Miss Lucy Bex found herself thinking how peaceful everything was. She did not, of course, mean the world at large, where the Russians were just beginning their great autumn advance and the British and Americans had landed in Sicily. Nor had she stopped caring about her nephew, Ivor, whom she had brought up, being away in the R.A.F. But at home, and in all her immediate surroundings, everything was unnaturally serene. Her brother Linnaeus, Ivor's father, for whom she kept house, and their elderly maid, Lizzie, were both well; she had made all her jam, within the limits of the sugar ration; thanks to the transport difficulties nobody was coming to stay, and she and Linnaeus were not having to bother about a summer holiday; it was the close season for charity, and the Flower Show was not for another fortnight. It was too good to last. It was the kind of vacuum nature abhorred. Something would be bound to happen.

Meanwhile it was not as if one had nothing in the world to do. The foregoing reflections were made in the course of cutting scabious and gypsophila and long purple plumes of Buddleia, for it was Saturday morning and Lucy's month to do the flowers in church. She put them in a basket, with seccateurs and a little cloth for mopping up water, because it was no use asking Duffy, the sexton, for anything, and set out by the shortcut through Beechfield.

As she crossed the gravel sweep from the front avenue of Beechfield to the back, Mrs. Nichol-Jervis came out on the steps.

"I am not coming to see you," said Lucy. "Only passing through."

"Good!" said Mrs. Nichol-Jervis. "I was afraid you had come to cry off for this afternoon. I'm rather counting on your support."

"Then Lady Madeleine Osmund is really coming?"

"They are all three coming, and Ernest simply must have another man."

"All right, I'll drag Linnaeus." Lucy knew her friend was under no illusions about her brother's willingness to go out to tea on Saturday afternoons. "Though I don't see why you have to have a men's four. It isn't tennis."

"Conversation is just as bad if the enemy are two to one. I forget whether you've met them all."

"Only Lady Madeleine. I've seen Mr. Osmund and the nephew once or twice in the bus. Don't you think the young man is very good-looking?"

"Yes, quite," replied Mrs. Nichol-Jervis, as casually as if she had not got a marriageable daughter.

"Wendy likes him, doesn't she?"

"She finds him useful as a partner."

"I expect he dances beautifully."

"So Wendy says."

It was, in fact, Wendy Nichol-Jervis who had introduced these titled exotics. Lady Madeleine's nephew was the grandson of the old Earl of Barna, by his first marriage, and was the present holder of the title. Wendy had met him in a hotel the summer before and had seen something of him in Dublin during the winter. He worked democratically in Mr. Osmund's office, lived in a flat in town, but spent his weekends with his relatives. So when Lady Madeleine Osmund and her husband came to live in Clonmeen, Mrs. Nichol-Jervis had some reason to call.

Lucy Bex had called too, though not without some hesitation. She was a little shy of an Earl's daughter, even one who was married to a commoner, but, as she pointed out to Linnaeus, they were going to be next door neighbors. Linnaeus said that only meant that, having called, she would not be able to avoid knowing them; it was safer to run such risks with people at a distance. But nobody minded Linnaeus, and, if the Osmunds were friends of the Nichol-Jervises, even he would have to nerve himself to social relations with them.

All the same, if she had not disapproved of Linnaeus's making such a pose of being unsociable, Lucy might have agreed with him in doubting if the Osmunds were quite in their line. Lady Madeleine was so very smart, by Clonmeen standards. As for the handsome Lord Barna, everybody knew that his mother had been a chorus girl, a *French* chorus girl. Whether he would strike Mrs. Nichol-Jervis as a nice young man for Wendy was more than Lucy had been able to guess. The entail was broken and the estates all sold, so he had nothing to recommend him but his title. But mothers can be funny about titles.

"Shall I tell you a little story," said Lucy suddenly, "about Lady Madeleine? It happened under my own eyes, and it would make a nice tidbit for the Miss Cuffes, but I shall only tell you."

The two ladies found themselves sitting on the wall of the stone steps, which was a convenient height for resting absentmindedly when you did not mean to settle.

"I was round the village yesterday," continued Lucy, putting her basket down in the shade, "and I called in at Dunne's for groceries, and

Lady Madeleine was there. She was paying her bill, so I sat down to wait while she wrote out a check. Matter of fact, I was hoping they'd let me have a little flake meal, if I waited till there was no one else in the shop."

"Did they?" asked Mrs. Nichol-Jervis.

"No, they hadn't any. We shan't see it now till the new harvest. Well, as I said, Lady Madeleine was making out a check, and she said to Mrs. Dunne, 'Look here, I've come out without any money, and I've got to go into town, and when the bus gets in it'll be too late for the bank. Could you possibly let me have five pounds, and I'll put it on to this check?' "

"Why not?" said Mrs. Nichol-Jervis.

"Wait now, till you hear. Well, you know Mrs. Dunne. She's the decentest sort in the world, and she wouldn't want to disoblige. She said, 'Certainly I will, my lady,' and she handed over four pounds ten in notes and ten shillings silver out of the till. And Lady Madeleine tore up her check and wrote a new one. But what I happened to notice—it was pure chance, though I know it does sound nosy—I happened to notice the date, and she'd made it a month ahead."

"Anybody could do that by mistake."

"They might," said Lucy, who was just a few years too old to say, "Sez you."

"I hope you didn't tell her!"

"Now really, what do you take me for?"

"Well, I don't see much in that," said Mrs. Nichol-Jervis.

"Well, I just thought it was interesting."

It was a difference that Lucy had often regretted between herself and her great friend, that Mrs. Nichol-Jervis was apt to be high-minded about gossip. She was an unimaginative person, and very well brought up; one might nearly as well talk to a man. Lucy believed in gossip, but not idle gossip. She practiced it as an art. This item, for instance, was the last thing she would have entrusted to any of the inveterate talkers of Clonmeen. But thinking it might be as well for Mrs. Nichol-Jervis to have an inkling of her new acquaintance's financial dealings, she had offered it to her as one student of human nature to another. She might have asked herself, "Is it true? Is it kind? Is it helpful?" and, except perhaps on the score of kindness, it would pass.

Whatever may be said against gossip on general principles, if Lucy Bex had not taken an interest in her neighbors, the wrong person might have been hanged when a murder was committed in Clonmeen. Not that she ever set up as a detective. Her brother, Linnaeus, had a mind soaked in crime by means of light reading, but Lucy herself preferred Jane Austen and Trollope. But when it came to uncovering a real crime in all its domestic details, Linnaeus had to admit that he was only Lucy's Watson. She never expected, nor even intended, to solve the mystery. The way it happened was that she could not help taking an interest, and then, as she explained to Detective Inspector Lancey, she suddenly woke up to the fact that something she knew, and the police did not, might have a vital bearing on the case.

As yet, however, the crime was only impending, only taking its cloudy shape in the mind of one still innocent of murder. A little disappointed at having her story fall flat, Lucy picked up her basket again.

"Those are pretty," said Mrs. Nichol-Jervis. "I like the Buddleia with the other pink and blue things. Shouldn't have thought of it myself. Tell me, are there any more developments about the Flower Show?"

Geographical nearness to Mrs. McGoldrick, who was the moving spirit of the Flower Show, had let Linnaeus Bex in for the post of Secretary. The Show was to be held at Annalee House. Such local visitations leave few homes unaffected. Mr. Nichol-Jervis was a Patron, and Wendy Nichol-Jervis was on the Teas, as was Lucy herself. As for Mrs. Nichol-Jervis, she was inclined to "enjoy ill health," and she brought staying out of things to a fine art.

"We've had a reply from Mr. O'Gallchobhair," said Lucy. "Such a nice letter, and he is going to open it."

"Is he indeed?"

"Don't raise your eyebrows at me. It's just what we want: publicity."

Mr. O'Gallchobhair was a popular member of the Dail of this period, who happened to live in Clonmeen. Neither the Nichol-Jervises nor the Bexes voted for his particular party, but Lucy was prepared to be deferential to any public man and thought they ought to make the most of him. Mrs. Nichol-Jervis refused to regard him as an asset. "Dragging in politics," she commented.

"Good-bye," said Lucy to that. And, having reproached Mrs. Nichol-Jervis with making her idle away half the morning, she moved away down the green shade of the back avenue leading to the church.

CHAPTER II
Talking of Poison

IT MIGHT seem nearly impossible to remember what people talked about at an average Clonmeen tea party, and certainly there was no very brilliant conversation at the Nichol-Jervises' that afternoon, but it was more interesting in the light of later events than at the time it took place.

Mrs. Nichol-Jervis's theory of hospitality was that, like bills, you paid it off periodically. She would wait till she owed several people invitations, and then give a party and ask them all back. Whether or not they were people who would get on with each other was left to chance. The entertainment provided was always the same: going round the garden.

The party which had been assembled on this occasion to meet the Osmunds was a fair cross section of Clonmeen gardening circles. Mrs. McGoldrick, an excellent, uninhibited woman, went in for bedding out and begonias and "choice blooms" in the more professional florist categories. Old Miss Milfoyle, on the other hand, was a retiring person with mainly antiquarian interests: a collector of old rose varieties and the "Irish" double primroses. The two Bexes liked to try new plants as well as old; their garden was a medley which polite visitors called "old world" when they meant "untidy." As for the Nichol-Jervises themselves, Mr. Nichol-Jervis dedicated himself mainly to gardening for the pot, i.e., to cultivating luscious fruit and vegetables in collaboration with an expert called Quin. It was another bond between the Nichol-Jervises and the Osmunds that Quin's son, Larry, had gone to be a gardener at Annalee Hall. In his lighter moments, Quin would also assist Mr. Nichol-Jervis to grow a few flowers for his own amusement.

Besides the Osmunds, who were late, there was one other stranger in the party. Miss Milfoyle had asked if she might bring her paying guest, a Miss FitzEustace, who was such a sweet woman. One new face would have been enough to enliven the gathering, for, since the laying up of cars, Clonmeen had been thrown on its own resources for society. Now there were going to be four, and Miss FitzEustace's sweetness would have been almost wasted if she had not had a private innings before the principal guests arrived.

Invitations on these occasions were for "between four and half-past," which everybody understood to mean twenty-five past four. Allowing for differences in their watches, the arrivals would be spread over ten minutes, during which the house parlormaid was kept busy. Having shut the door on the final guest, she would then hasten up the tea. After tea there would be ample time to go round the garden. But the timing was upset by the lateness of the Osmunds. Mrs. Nichol-Jervis sat wondering how long to wait, and all the other ladies, sympathizing with her predicament, industriously made conversation, while the men fidgeted and kept comparing their watches with the clock.

Luckily there was the Flower Show to talk about. The Bexes gave the news of Mr. O'Gallchobhair's letter, and Mrs. McGoldrick capped it by announcing that she had successfully negotiated for the Clonmeen Brass and Reed Band. Everybody hoped Miss FitzEustace was staying on for the show, and Miss FitzEustace assured everybody that she was.

"Have you thought of having a class for wildflowers?" Miss FitzEustace asked. "To the seeing eye, a common dandelion is as beautiful as a chrysanthemum."

"Somehow," said Lucy Bex, "I don't think you can be a gardener."

It then came out that Miss FitzEustace was something much rarer in Clonmeen: an artist. She specialized in painting garden scenes and spent much of her time visiting with people who commissioned her to paint and invited her to stay. So that although she had never had a garden of her own, she could talk gardening with anybody, and had also a fund of country house small talk that made her quite an acquisition.

"We were saying as we came up the drive," remarked Miss Milfoyle guilelessly to Mrs. Nichol-Jervis, "that Miss FitzEustace really ought to paint your beautiful beech trees."

Mrs. Nichol-Jervis inquired in an undertone whether Miss FitzEustace was very badly off, and looked relieved to hear that she had private means. The walls of Beechfield were already well covered with works by artists of two classes: some were relatives or connections of the family, others had been recommended to them as deserving cases. The Nichol-Jervises may have been dimly aware that there were other reasons for buying pictures, but they did not take them seriously. Not being a widow or crippled, Miss FitzEustace stood little chance.

She herself, meanwhile, was chatting away amiably to Lucy and Mrs. McGoldrick about gardens she had painted. Countess Marioff, whose daughters were the year's two most striking brides, had the charming idea of giving each of them a picture of her old home to hang in her new one. The Gore-Hartys, the well-known racing and hunting people, were taking to gardening in their old age, and had asked her to paint their place, Mount Music, before they started alterations, with a prospect of another commission to paint a companion picture when they had finished. Old Lady Mossbanks had had her down several times to paint all her gardens at Moss Park in their proper seasons: there was the Dutch Bulb Garden, the Rhododendron Walk, the Rose Garden, and she was going back in November to do the Chrysanthemum House. In a case like that, Miss FitzEustace explained, she reduced her usual charge of thirty guineas a picture, and accepted a hundred guineas for the set of four.

Bearing up as well as she could against this impressive catalogue, Lucy Bex said she supposed Miss Fitz-Eustace had come to Clonmeen for a rest and a change. To which the artist replied, "Well, a change, anyway," leaving it to be inferred that she was open to commissions if anybody felt like it.

Just then, nobody did. What they all wanted more and more was their tea. Wendy Nichol-Jervis wore an apologetic expression, as if to say, "Don't hold me responsible," for she was conscious of the newcomers being generally regarded as her property, though she hardly knew them, except Roland (Roland was Lord Barna). This was not the first time Wendy had felt it to be a doubtful experiment, introducing one's young men into one's home circle.

The drawing-room clock tactlessly chimed five.

"By the way," said Miss FitzEustace, as if it was an entirely new idea, "aren't you expecting Lady Madeleine Osmund?"

"I was," replied Mrs. Nichol-Jervis. "Do you know Lady Madeleine?"

"Not exactly," replied Miss FitzEustace, "but I was rather hoping to meet her."

"I'm afraid something must have happened to her."

"Mummy," said Wendy soothingly, "shall I tell them to send up tea? The Osmunds may be here by the time it arrives." Without waiting for her mother to make up her mind, she walked over to the door, and then, to her relief, she saw through the window that they were coming up the drive. A minute or two later the house parlormaid, perplexed by the titles, announced,

"Mr. and Lady Osmund, ma'am, and Lord Barna."

Lady Madeleine Osmund walked in, and all of a sudden the

drawing room smelled like the Carnation Classes under canvas on a hot day. She was herself something of an exhibition bloom; at least, she cultivated her appearance with a care that Clonmeen ladies only bestowed on their plants. Her complexion was as flawless as one of Mrs. McGoldrick's prize-winning roses ("The whole secret," Mrs. McGoldrick had been telling Mr. Nichol-Jervis, "is to give a good mulch.") and she would no more have missed her regular hair set than Lucy Bex would have failed to water the tomatoes. Her clothes were simple in an expensive way; they had no competition to fear from the Clonmeen ladies' re-blocked straw hats and homemade art-silk frocks or out-of-date tailormades. Lady Madeleine's eye passed over them rapidly, only pausing a shade longer at Wendy Nichol-Jervis, for Wendy was lissome in linen and, in a young, spontaneous way, a bit of a beauty.

Mr. Osmund, a mid-middle-aged man in a city suit, hovered behind his wife like a dim figure sketched into the background of a fashion plate. But it was the young Earl of Barna, though his entrance was unobtrusive, who caused the greatest flutter. Young men are rarities in Clonmeen, but young men as good-looking as Lord Barna are rarities everywhere; you had to grant him a right to elegance which, in somebody less handsome, would have been taken for vanity. Yet he was unassuming, and had sufficient poise to look at home in even less accustomed surroundings than a Clonmeen tea party. On catching Lucy Bex's eye (for she was gazing at him), he gave her a disarming smile, and she quite blushed, she felt so gratified.

"I told you so, Madeleine," Mr. Osmund was saying, "I said we should be late." Lady Madeleine exclaimed at Mrs. Nichol-Jervis for not having had tea. "I never dreamed you would be waiting for us. You must be simply dying of thirst. I know how people miss their tea. Actually, Otway and I never have it at home—just a cocktail or something if we feel like it."

"I'm afraid we never have cocktails," said Mrs. Nichol-Jervis. "My husband does not care about them. But tea is ready now, so shall we go in?"

With some hesitation and ceremony at the door, the party was transferred to the dining-room. Tea (wholemeal bread and honey, with a large plain cake of flour which the cook had illegally sifted to a prewar whiteness) was laid on an oval mahogany table, round a centerpiece of roses in a silver bowl. The table was large enough for all the company to sit round. Mrs. Nichol-Jervis saw Lady Madeleine seated on her husband's right, and Mr. Osmund on her own, and allowed the rest to place themselves. Miss FitzEustace was thus able to take advantage of a general backwardness and seat herself next to Lady Madeleine, who seemed to have a fascination for her.

However, Miss FitzEustace could not expect to have the principal guest all to herself. There arose a kind of competition for her between the artist and Mrs. McGoldrick, with Mr. Nichol-Jervis as a runner-up. Mr. Nichol-Jervis wanted to advise a newcomer to the fold on what needed doing in her garden. Mrs. McGoldrick was determined to secure some entries for the Flower Show.

"The fruit trees have been very much let go," said Mr. Nichol-Jervis. "There's a big job of pruning to be done on the apple trees, as I can see from the road. You'd better get Larry Quin on to them when the time comes. Those trees are a very awkward proposition. They should never have been let grow so big."

"Ah, you gardeners!" chimed in Miss FitzEustace. "Always pruning and cutting. Now I like a tree that I can sit under."

"Well, so do I," declared Lady Madeleine. "It was the apple trees I fell for when we came in the spring. The blossom was too marvelous. I shall keep them just as they are, but there are plenty of other things to be done. I want a swimming pool, and a water garden, and a rockery. What I feel is, the whole place is too dead level. Can any of you recommend a good landscape gardener?"

The Clonmeen people had no suggestions to offer. They had all laid out their own gardens, or continued them on the lines planned by their forebears. Lucy Bex asked Mr. Osmund if he was interested in gardening. He had been listening to his wife, and replied,

"What's that? Oh, er, yes, to a certain extent."

"Don't believe him!" called Lady Madeleine from the other end of the table. "He couldn't be less interested in getting anything done at the Hall. All he does is to keep fussing about the cost."

"Somebody must," said Mr. Osmund, in a hollow voice like Hamlet's ghost.

"But no matter what you spend on a garden," cooed Miss FitzEustace, "it will repay you a hundredfold."

"Exactly what I tell him!" cried Lady Madeleine. "And look what we save by living here instead of in Merrion Square. But when I agreed to come and retrench at Annalee Hall, I never meant to live in it just as it was."

In a pause, while the Clonmeen people assimilated the idea that Annalee Hall appeared to its new inhabitants in the light of a country cottage, Miss FitzEustace seized the chance to tell Lady Madeleine about the alterations carried out by the Gore-Hartys, who had commissioned two companion pictures of the garden before and after. Mr. Nichol-Jervis listened with politely concealed impatience, but when the artist stopped to refuel with bread and honey, it was Mrs. McGoldrick who got in first.

Lady Madeleine had somehow managed to escape hearing about the Flower Show and inquired when and where it was.

"Not that we have anything," she said. "We're simply a wilderness. Tell you what I'll do if you like. I'll open it for you. I'm frightfully good at opening functions."

"Now isn't that too bad?" said Mrs. McGoldrick, really disappointed. "I'm afraid we've got somebody else. Mr. Bex has just got a promise out of the T.D. down the road here. You see, some of the committee thought it would be nice to have a celebrity."

Only one person laughed, and that was Lord Barna. Lady Madeleine did not seem to see anything wrong with this remark and graciously said she hoped Mrs. McGoldrick would send her a copy of the Schedule. This had, of course, been done once already, but it is easy for such things to get overlooked.

Satisfied, for the time being, with this degree of encouragement (she still intended to ask for a subscription at a more private moment), Mrs. McGoldrick turned her fire on the Nichol-Jervises.

It was she who brought up the subject of the Arabian monkshood, an uncommon variety of a plant which was common enough in Clonmeen as elsewhere, but which, in the course of the next few weeks, was to be rigorously weeded out from most of the gardens round about. But as yet, although all these gardeners were aware of the plant's dangerous properties, it had not acquired a sinister significance.

"Oh, Mrs. Nichol-Jervis," said Mrs. McGoldrick. "I've been wanting to ask you, couldn't you put up a 'not for competition' exhibit of those plants from the Middle East? That interesting monkshood, for instance."

"But it looks just like an ordinary monkshood," objected Mrs. Nichol-Jervis. "Rather a poor one at that."

"Then what's the point about it?" asked Lady Madeleine.

Several people were able to inform her, for everybody who had been round Beechfield that summer had been shown the collection of plants that Mrs. Nichol-Jervis had raised from seed that her son in the Ninth Army had sent home.

"*Aconitum ferox,* is it not?" said Linnaeus Bex.

"Yes," said Wendy. "I expect that's because it's ferociously poisonous."

Linnaeus pointed out that all monkshoods were poisonous. "Aconitine comes under the Poisons Act, Schedule A, Part I. You'd have no end of red tape over buying it in a shop, but anybody can grow it in their garden."

"Well anyhow," Wendy insisted, "this monkshood's the one that's used by the Arabs for executing criminals. They make it into a drug called bish."

"Spelt B-I-K-H," added her father.

Some people looked impressed and others skeptical. It was odd to remember afterwards how cheerfully they went on discussing poison over the teacups.

"Well, it's just that sort of thing we want," said Mrs. McGoldrick, "if you could write that down and put a card beside the vase. So educational for the school children."

"Simple lessons in Home Murder," said Linnaeus.

"My dear mother," said Miss Milfoyle, "would never allow us to grow monkshood in the garden at home, though I have always rather liked it. It is such a quaint, old-world plant."

"The old world," said Linnaeus, "was not all it's cracked up to be."

"Are you thinking of the monks or the poisons?" smiled Mrs. Nichol-Jervis. She was enjoying the respite that comes to a hostess after dealing with the second cups, and now she began to catch people's eyes to see if they were ready to make a move. They had to wait, however, while Mr. Nichol-Jervis worked off his opinions on apple trees.

"I consider standards unpractical," he informed Lady Madeleine, "but there is no reason why they should not bear you a good crop. The higher branches may be awkward to get at, but Larry Quin could get a loan of his father's long pruning ladder. It's a very handy type of ladder for the purpose, with a top tapered to fit in the fork of an outer branch. Larry understands pruning all right. I trained him myself. You need not be afraid to let him loose. That is"—Mr. Nichol-Jervis recollected a minor detail—"if he's still with you."

"Why shouldn't Larry be with us?" asked Osmund.

"I heard he was applying for a permit."

"Surely I told you, Otway," said Lady Madeleine, in the defensive voice of one who knew she hadn't. "Larry did say something to me about going to England, but I said we couldn't spare him, and that was that."

"I never heard a word about it." Osmund looked very much annoyed. "You ought to have sent him to me. Do you mean, you said we wouldn't let him go?"

"Of course I did. Why, if Larry went, the cook would go too. They're walking out, you know."

It was natural for Larry Quin to be tempted by the high wages offered for war work in England. The only obstacle to his departure was the form of enquiries which would be sent to his employer, before the authorities would let a young agricultural laborer leave the country. A sympathetic employer might stretch a point and say "No," to questions like, "Did the applicant refuse an offer of employment with you?" and "Have you any employment immediately available for him?" But it seemed that Lady Madeleine could not tell a lie.

"I shouldn't dare insist on keeping somebody who wanted to go away," murmured Miss Milfoyle. "Won't you find it a little embarrassing?"

"Oh, we can make it up to him by raising his wages," said Lady Madeleine carelessly. This brought a snort of protest from Mr. Osmund. Lucy Bex had been watching his expression with fascination. She thought that if he had been corked, the cork would have popped.

But he only said mildly, "The way I look at it is, ought we to keep a young fellow back from the war effort? What do you say, Jervis?"

But Mrs. Nichol-Jervis thought the conversation had gone far enough. A little more and it would be a political discussion. She signaled firmly to Lucy Bex, and together they stood up. It was time to take the party round the garden.

CHAPTER III
Going Round the Garden

GOING ROUND a garden is a serious performance, almost a rite. You are not supposed to wander at will; the owner is sure to have his planned itinerary. You must know how slowly to move, when to pause and gaze, enraptured, at a vista, and when to stoop down, put on spectacles, and peer minutely at some individual plant. All that was second nature to the Clonmeen contingent, but the other elements in the party were inclined to be unmanageable. Lord Barna and Wendy — "the children"—slipped away together. Otway Osmund tagged along meekly at the rear of the main procession, but Lady Madeleine and Miss FitzEustace, finding the tempo too slow for them, walked briskly on ahead. They were deep in conversation: Lady Madeleine, no doubt, was telling Miss FitzEustace all about her projected improvements to the Hall, and Miss FitzEustace was comparing them to those carried out by the Gore-Hartys, with special reference to the interest of having a pictorial record. But Mr. Nichol-Jervis suddenly noticed them heading toward a June border that had gone over, and called after them, luring back his principal guest with an offer of plants.

The party moved slower than ever then, because they had to stop not only at rare plants but also at commoner ones that were thriving enough for Mr. Nichol-Jervis to spare Lady Madeleine bits. It gave him as much pleasure as anything in gardening to ensure that some of his pet plants, which were due to be divided anyway, would find scope in another garden and spare him the heartrending effort of throwing them out. So he kept on happily loading more and more clumps of roots and earth into a basket, which Otway Osmund had to carry. Lady Madeleine was getting something for nothing, which was enough to keep her happy, but some of the veteran gardeners grew a little restive, Miss FitzEustace felt frustrated, and Mrs. Nichol-Jervis became absentminded, wondering what had happened to Lord Barna and Wendy.

When at last they came on "the children" again, they found them innocently engaged in eating green figs off a tree on the wall. It was an occupation that won Mrs. Nichol-Jervis's approval. She pressed green figs on everybody, both to eat there and to take away. Some hesitated.

"Yes, I know," said Mrs. Nichol-Jervis frankly. "That's why I want to get rid of them. We have such quantities, and Ernest will eat them."

"He likes them but they don't like him," said Miss Milfoyle understandingly.

Mr. Nichol-Jervis protested that it wasn't the figs, it was the bread, which was a good bid for sympathy, because the brown emergency bread was generally unpopular. But his wife replied,

"That's all very well, Ernest, but bread or no bread, you were all right last year."

"Why last year?" asked Lord Barna.

"The whole crop was stolen," said Mrs. Nichol-Jervis, "and really, I was thankful."

There was a chorus of protest from the assembled garden owners. Nobody has such a keen sense of property as the person who grows it himself. They all began to talk about depredations made on their own gardens: wall-trained trees broken down by people climbing over, and apples and pears stolen weeks before they would be ripe. Now, vegetables were being taken too. Everybody agreed that it was getting worse since the war.

"It used to be only boys out for a lark," said Mr. Nichol-Jervis, "but now it's organized crime."

Linnaeus Bex could not resist adding,

"Common or garden crime."

"But they won't get away with it here," Mr. Nichol-Jervis went on. "Look!" He pointed to an angle of the wall where a tree on the far side provided an easy way of climbing over. The top of the wall was all sticky and glistening with a recent coat of tar.

"They'll spoil their clothes on that," said Mr. Nichol-Jervis with satisfaction, "and we'll have a clue to identity, if the Guards get a move on."

The tar was easily the most popular exhibit of the garden tour. Everybody hailed the idea as brilliant, and those who had also suffered from garden thefts determined to copy it. Things looked bad for local lawbreakers, with even old Miss Milfoyle breathing venom and hoping the Guards would catch somebody and make an example of them.

"Bikh would be too good for them," laughed Lord Barna. "By the way, Wendy, you never showed it to me."

"Why, there it is." Wendy pointed to a nearby clump of dark blue-flowered spikes. The *Aconitum ferox* is lower growing than the best garden monkshoods, and not at all impressive. They all looked at it respectfully.

"Want some?" Wendy asked the Earl.

"No thanks," he smiled, "I have no murderous intentions."

"Well, if you develop any, you know where to come."

"I'll be coming anyway," he assured her.

By now the August afternoon was mellowing round them. Lit by a sinking sun, the Beechfield garden was at one of its loveliest hours. The tea party had reached the stage when everybody can relax. Having performed the compulsory tour, and knowing that politeness no longer constrained them to stay, the guests found more and more to interest them.

As they drifted toward the house, Lady Madeleine was again monopolized by Miss FitzEustace; Miss Milfoyle, walking with the two Bexes, asked for the latest news of Ivor; Mrs. McGoldrick kept her eyes open for possible Flower Show entries, which she pointed out to the Nichol-Jervises; Wendy and Lord Barna did not seem to have exhausted their conversational resources. Only Mr. Osmund was a little neglected and loitered behind the others carrying the heavy basket.

Gradually the scattered groups converged on the conservatory steps. And there, to top off the afternoon's entertainment, the news leaked out that Miss FitzEustace was going to paint Lady Madeleine.

This gave the general satisfaction that people of goodwill experience at seeing anybody put through a deal, besides the excitement of being present at the genesis of a work of art. Miss Milfoyle was delighted at having brought her p.g. into touch with a new patron. Mrs. Nichol-Jervis said it was a charming idea, and added in a whisper to Lucy Bex, "I was so afraid we should have her painting here."

It must be admitted that Lady Madeleine's own family showed somewhat less enthusiasm. Lord Barna took her on one side and murmured reproachfully.

"Why didn't you tell me you had this yen for being painted? I could have put you on to a chap—"

"No, thank you," retorted Lady Madeleine. "Your chap would give me two profiles and a green nose."

"No, he wouldn't. He's a first-rate man at a straight portrait. He's a coming genius, in fact."

"I suppose you owe him money. Anyway, this isn't a portrait, it's a picture of the garden, with me in it to make it interesting. And she must be good, look what she charges."

"Have you asked old Otway ?"

"Ssh!" said Lady Madeleine. "It's a surprise. A birthday present."

"What! Do you mean you're going to pay for it?"

"Of course. You needn't look at me like that."

But on Mr. Osmund's coming up, he had already been congratulated on his prospective acquisition, and the surprise was given away. On the whole he bore up well, only saying that he should have thought they had enough photographs of his wife already. Lady Madeleine looked a little put out and repeated that the picture was to be a birthday present.

"How like you, Madeleine!" Osmund replied. It might have been intended for gratitude.

Miss FitzEustace and Lady Madeleine then became involved in arrangements, which ended in Miss FitzEustace promising to start work next morning at eleven, Sunday though it was, as that seemed to be Lady Madeleine's least occupied day.

Meanwhile the other guests began saying good-bye, though in a lingering fashion. After all, a tea party in time of emergency was not achieved without the expenditure of fuel for baking, and of rationed tea, butter and sugar. It was necessary to show appreciation of the Nichol-Jervises' sacrifices. The air was musical with civilities. But they took themselves away at last, the Annalee Hall party last of all, with Lord Barna behind, taking his turn to carry the basket of plants.

Wendy and her father stood and waved till they had all disappeared round the curve of the avenue. Mrs. Nichol-Jervis went to lie down in the peace of having done her duty.

CHAPTER IV
Common or Garden Crime

THE CRIME WAVE, or what counted as such in Clonmeen, was on. The rest of the green figs disappeared from Beechfield that same night. Lucy and Linnaeus heard all about it on Sunday morning, when, according to custom, they called for the Nichol-Jervises on their way to church.

Mr. Nichol-Jervis had discovered the loss on his morning round of the garden after breakfast. He had rung up the Civic Guards and particularly instructed them to look out for traces of tar on the clothes of the Houlihans or the Slatterys, two neighboring families who were automatically suspected in any case of this kind.

"But today they'll be wearing their Sunday blues," Mrs. Nichol-Jervis reminded him.

"I said, 'Look at their hands too.' They won't get rid of that stuff so easily. If the Guards know their job they ought to nail somebody this time, and I hope they'll catch it from the D. J. Little devils: they tore up some of the monkshood too."

"Was that all?" asked Linnaeus Bex. "I mean," he corrected himself, as

Mr. Nichol-Jervis glared at him, "it was quite enough, of course. I only hoped you'd been spared any more extensive damage."

"No, it was a tip and run business. It always is. But, damn it! That's two years running I've barely tasted my own fig crop."

"He only had about two dozen yesterday," Mrs. Nichol-Jervis confided to Lucy, "what with those he ate in the morning and after lunch before you all came. That's partly what's the matter with him."

"You are able to be philosophic about it," said Lucy, amused.

"Oh, I am quite resigned, I assure you. Though, I must say, it was very odd about the monkshood." Mrs. Nichol-Jervis looked thoughtful.

"Odd? Not a bit," barked her husband. "Just shows you what they are. 'There's a pretty flower, let's grub it up!' That's the mentality."

"I'm afraid Ernest isn't in a very Sunday frame of mind," said Mrs. Nichol-Jervis. "Let us hope church will do him good."

Church attendance that morning was thinned by the fine weather. One of the absentees was Wendy, who had pleaded that her Cairn terrier, Mack, needed exercise. Mr. Osmund and Lord Barna could hardly be called absentees, as they never came. Lady Madeleine came sometimes—she said it kept one in touch—but she was sitting for Miss FitzEustace, and Miss FitzEustace was painting Lady Madeleine. Miss Milfoyle was late because, just as she was about to start, the house parlormaid at Annalee Hall had telephoned to say that Miss FitzEustace would be staying there to lunch. This put Miss Milfoyle out, as she had ordered a regular Sunday dinner for her paying guest and did not feel like tackling a joint by herself. But Lady Madeleine did not care how many Miss Milfoyles she upset in her course through life.

The third person to have her Sunday frame of mind disturbed was Lucy Bex. It was only a trifle, but irritating: somebody had been fiddling with her flowers. As soon as she looked at the two altar vases which she had arranged the day before, she noticed that the left-hand one was fuller than the right. Lucy hated crowded arrangements; she fancied that flowers liked plenty of air all round them. Then she discovered that what had been added to her own mixed bouquet was a heavy spike of monkshood. A short, squat monkshood, with a habit of growth similar to the plant that they had been shown at Beechfield.

This made a little mystery to puzzle over all through the service. Who could have put the flower there? Could it be the identical monkshood which had been uprooted from Beechfield? If so, it ought to provide a clue to the taker of the green figs, and the Nichol-Jervises ought to be interested. Lucy glanced round at them—they sat across the aisle and farther back—they were looking quite calm and Christian, but perhaps they had not noticed.

These cogitations distracted Lucy's attention from the sermon, though it was an impressive one. Canon Gowler dealt that morning with the uncertainty of life and the vanity of human expectations, basing his theme on the newspapers, but clothing it in something like the phraseology of his favorite seventeenth-century authors. Old Miss Milfoyle, who did not like to be found wanting in a Biblical reference, was set hunting through Ecclesiastics for a quotation from Sir Thomas Browne. The concluding hymn, "Brief life is here our portion," carried the same message. But none of the congregation seemed unduly oppressed by a sense of mortality as they filed out into the August sunshine.

Lucy walked on ahead with Mrs. Nichol-Jervis and promptly ascertained that she *had* noticed the monkshood. She, too, thought it looked like their own Asiatic variety.

"Shall we go back and make sure?" Lucy suggested. "Duffy should know who brought it into church, and then we can ask them where they found it."

"But I had much rather not know," said Mrs. Nichol-Jervis. "It might end with Ernest bringing somebody to Court, and that would be so upsetting. Luckily Ernest himself never notices the flowers, even when you do them, and I don't see any point in mentioning it." So Lucy had to contain her curiosity for the time being.

When the churchgoers came out of the Beechfield back avenue on to the gravel sweep, they found Wendy on the steps talking to Lord Barna. The young man and girl, both so good-looking, with Wendy's dog and the stately old house in the background, made a charming picture, at any rate by magazine cover standards. Whether it was a picture that appealed to Mrs. Nichol-Jervis, Lucy could not decide.

Wendy was in high spirits. She waved to the church party, and called, "Hello, good morning! Mack and I met Roland, Mother, and we all went for a walk together."

Lord Barna said, "Wendy thought I needed exercising too."

"Of course you do," said Wendy. "He's in town all the week, you know," she explained to the Bexes, as if it was the most dreadful fate. "He only comes up to breathe at weekends."

"Where did you take him?" asked Lucy.

Clonmeen is not a good district for walks, as high stone walls round private property shut off the roads from the view.

"Oh, we climbed the walls," said Lord Barna, "and jumped the ditches, and paddled through the streams. When Wendy goes for a walk, she goes for a walk. Look at Mack, he's flat out."

The Cairn terrier was lying down, looking profoundly bored after a morning of playing gooseberry. His mistress said complacently," Well, I think I did a good morning's work, and now I'm starving."

"Come in and have your dinner, then," said Mrs. Nichol-Jervis. It was desirable to get Sunday dinner over in good time to let the Beechfield cook go out. She did not invite Lord Barna to join them. She might have been afraid of upsetting Lady Madeleine.

"See you some time," said Wendy to Roland.

"You'll see me tomorrow evening."

"So I will. Mother, Roland and I have a theater date."

"Mind you're there on time," said Lord Barna.

"Same to you. Good-bye."

The Nichol-Jervis family went indoors. The two Bexes and the Earl of Barna strolled on down the front drive. Lucy was sorry that they only had a short way to go, as she wanted to investigate Wendy's young man. He looked as elegant as ever this morning, making one think of greyhounds and racehorses. His walk had only disheveled him to the extent of dusty shoes and a damp lock of hair on his forehead. Thinking how completely he seemed a young man of leisure, she asked him if he found it trying to spend the summer working in town.

"Oh, well—" he said, and left it at that.

"Accountancy, isn't it?" said Linnaeus. "An excellent mental training."

"You think so, sir?" said Lord Barna, in a voice of courteous dissent. Linnaeus winced at the "sir"; it was not so many years since he had called people "sir" himself. But Lucy thought it was rather sweet.

"Don't you want to be a chartered accountant?" she asked.

"Might as well do that as anything else," he replied, with a shrug. "What I really want to do is hopeless."

"And what is that?"

"Dance," he said. And launched forthwith into an account of a ballet society of which he was the secretary, cofounder, and moving spirit. It was national, it was continental; it was rooted in the people, it was sophisticated; it was a team, it was full of original geniuses; it carried on the purest ballet traditions, and it was developing completely along lines of its own. It was the only live artistic movement in Dublin.. Also Lucy remembered that she had actually heard of it, and had once nearly gone to a matinee of one of its productions, only it cleared up and she went to the zoo instead.

If she had gone, she would have had the pleasure of seeing Lord Barna dance a *pas seul* of his own devising. "It was really a piece of miming," he informed her, "based on an old street ballad. All about a man who is on his way to be hanged."

Lucy said she was sorry to have missed that. "Perhaps you'll do it again some time." He promised to let her know.

They had come right through the long tunnel of beech trees that was the front avenue and reached the imposing iron gates. There was a lodge with a smell of dinner cooking, to sharpen their appetites for lunch, and Linnaeus grew fidgety when Lucy and the Earl still loitered talking. Lucy asked if Lady Madeleine was interested in ballet. Lord Barna thought not.

"Not *really* interested. She gives a subscription and comes to some of the shows, but it's all partly to annoy old Otway. Otway takes a very poor view. I expect you've gathered, he's the complete Philistine."

"Oh, is he?"

"He doesn't know much about art, but he knows what he doesn't like. Accountancy is his idea of the good life, and he thinks I won't pass my finals."

"Wouldn't that be a pity?"

"I suppose it would. Especially from his point of view, because, you see, he's paid all my fees so far."

"But I am sure you will pass, won't you?" said. Lucy, with a well-meaning woman's faith in the power of suggestion.

Linnaeus resorted to taking out his watch. Lord Barna glanced at his own wrist and exclaimed, "My God!" With a characteristically graceful farewell gesture, between a wave and a salute, he set off rapidly for Annalee Hall.

"What an interesting boy!" said Lucy, looking after him. "I wonder where he went to school. I wonder whether he's older or younger than Ivor."

"All I wonder about him," said Linnaeus, "is why he isn't in the army. It'd do him a power of good."

CHAPTER V
Next Door to Death

MONDAY WAS the August bank holiday, a day off for Linnaeus Bex, who ordinarily went into Dublin to attend to the family business of selling scientific apparatus. Lucy, too, was more free than usual, with the meals ordered and no shopping to do. When she had tidied the bedrooms, which were her share of the morning housework, there was nothing to keep her from the garden.

She went first to the stable yard, to a loose box where they kept things like soot, kindlings, firebricks, lengths of lead piping, zinc gutters, odd wheels, wire, tins of this and that, including, sure enough, the end of a tin of tar. Armed with the last item, and with the small garden steps, she made for the part of the wall where little boys could climb over and proceeded to make it sticky for them. While doing this she commanded a view of the road to Annalee Hall and so was in a position to greet Miss FitzEustace when the artist appeared from that direction.

"Good morning, Miss FitzEustace!" Lucy called. "Isn't it a lovely day for the holiday?"

It was natural for Miss FitzEustace to look surprised at being addressed from the top of a wall, especially as she had only met Lucy once and had not known where she lived. But she gave a most violent start and stood gazing upwards quite blankly. Lucy thought it was odd for such a busy and lively person to be so slow in adjusting herself.

"But I suppose it isn't a holiday for you," Lucy chatted on, "if you're going to paint Lady Madeleine Osmund."

"Oh, Miss Bex," said Miss FitzEustace, recognizing her, "I wasn't expecting—you must excuse me—I've had rather a shock." She sounded out of breath. She came close to the bottom of the wall, and, in a lowered voice, told her news.

"Lady Madeleine's dead."

"Lady Madeleine!" repeated Lucy. "You can't mean Lady Madeleine Osmund. Why, she was perfectly well on Saturday."

" 'In the midst of life—' "

"But what happened to her?"

"That's the terrible part of it. She was poisoned."

"Good heavens! But you don't mean—of course it was an accident?"

"Oh yes, it was an accident. She wasn't the kind of person to commit suicide, was she? Not that you can always tell. But it was something she ate yesterday for lunch."

"Good heavens!" said Lucy again, and in her mind she nervously reviewed her own recent meals. They had all been simple and wholesome, but she felt a little dizzy and dripped tar on her overall without noticing.

"How did you hear about it?" she asked.

"I went up there this morning, to paint," Miss FitzEustace explained, "and I found the police in charge. I only saw one of the Guards. Naturally, I came away at once. I shall have to go back sometime, though, because I left my easel and paints there, which is just what would happen. I don't suppose they'll want that picture now," Miss FitzEustace sighed. "But in the presence of a great loss one ought not to think of one's own disappointments."

"I suppose there'll be an inquest," Lucy remarked.

"Oh yes." Miss FitzEustace looked aggrieved. "The Guard told me I might have to give evidence."

"You? But why?"

"Why, you see, I was there when it happened. When she was taken ill, I mean. I was there lunching with them yesterday. Indeed, I may have had a narrow escape myself."

Lucy saw that there was a lot more to tell, and it seemed to her that Miss FitzEustace would be the better for a sit-down, so at this point she invited her to come in. Miss FitzEustace hesitated, and thought she ought to hurry back and tell Miss Milfoyle, but that was another twenty minutes' walk, and the sun was now getting hot, and Lucy said she was just going to have elevenses. Lucy came down from her ladder and brought her guest in through the yard to the little back parlor giving on the garden, where she and Linnaeus mostly sat.

The elevenses were not a habit with Lucy, but had been invented to suit the occasion. What to produce was the problem. It was too hot for coffee, and anyhow the kitchen fire was out for fuel economy. Milk seemed cheerless, there was no lemonade or lime juice, and the beer they kept for Linnaeus hardly seemed suitable. Then Lucy bethought her of some homemade apple wine and brought in a bottle of it with two port glasses and some biscuits.

She found Miss FitzEustace recovering her normal cheerfulness. The

Bexes' garden room had a pleasant atmosphere; rugs, chintzes, book bindings, and photographs of Ivor, all faded into mellowness, made a favorable background for cozy chats. The bottle uncorked with a promising pop, and the two ladies sat sipping their wine in a genteelly Victorian manner. Presently Linnaeus, who had heard the cork pop, appeared outside the French windows. Lucy made a face at him to go away and thought he had taken the hint, but he had only gone to fetch a glass for himself. They had to make him understand that it was a funeral and not a wedding feast. Then he looked decorous, helped himself, refilled Miss FitzEustace's glass, and asked her to go back to the beginning.

"You stayed to dinner with the Osmunds," Lucy prompted.

"I did," said Miss FitzEustace, warming to her audience. "Or to lunch, I should say, because it was all cold. They have their Sunday dinner on Saturday night, and then on Sunday they don't heat up the oven at all. Such a good idea, don't you think? Because, really, in this weather, one would rather not have a hot meal in the middle of the day. Though I don't know whether they have the same joint again at night, or what."

Interesting as these domestic details were to anybody trying to manage on the same fuel ration, Linnaeus brushed them aside as irrelevant. It was Lucy who recognized, later, that the sequence of Saturday night dinner and Sunday lunch might have significance. But this was not till the inquest had brought out more facts.

Great talkers, like athletes and virtuosos in other lines, have to play themselves in. Miss FitzEustace's way of doing it was to spread herself on details. She went on,

"Though you mustn't take that to mean that there wasn't plenty to eat. The joint and salad and cold gooseberry pie to follow, and coffee afterwards in the garden. Quite simple, you see, and we were just a simple family party: Mr. Osmund and Lady Madeleine and Lord Barna and me."

"It sounds harmless enough," said Lucy, privately thinking that it sounded very dull food for a guest. "When was Lady Madeleine taken ill?"

"Over the coffee. She made it herself in a Cona, and just after she'd had her first cup she said she felt queer. She said she had an extraordinary sensation as if she was tingling all over. Then she felt giddy, and Mr. Osmund helped her indoors to lie down. That was when I thought I'd better come away."

"Then do you think it was something in the coffee?" asked Lucy.

"Hardly," put in Linnaeus. "Unless it was something exceptionally rapid. It would be more likely to be something she had taken beforehand. I mean, before lunch. A pill, or a cocktail, or something."

"Well, nobody offered me a cocktail," said Miss FitzEustace, "and I didn't see any signs of anything medicinal. I should have, because we went upstairs together to wash our hands. The wastepipe of the handbasin happened to be stopped up, and Lady Madeleine called the housemaid and scolded her about it. Of course she might have taken a pill unobtrusively, but she was so annoyed about the handbasin I don't believe she would have thought of it. And yet, I suppose it must have been something like that, because we all ate the same lunch, and the rest of us are still alive. Or do you think"—a look of horror overspread her face—"that it could have delayed effects?"

"Quite safe after twenty-four hours," Linnaeus assured her. Miss FitzEustace did a mental calculation and said it was twenty-one hours now since the beginning of yesterday's lunch. Linnaeus poured her out some more apple wine as an antidote.

Lucy said, "Tell me again exactly what you did have."

"Cold roast beef and potato salad, and then the gooseberry pie to follow. There wasn't enough sugar with the gooseberries, as often happens nowadays, and they set my teeth on edge. I certainly blamed the gooseberries when Lady Madeleine felt ill, but could a person die of them?"

"Perhaps she was allergic to them."

"Then why eat them?"

"People will, you know. Like Mr. Nichol-Jervis and the figs. Though you wouldn't expect gooseberries to be as much of a temptation."

"What did you drink?" asked Linnaeus with interest.

"They had lager beer, and I drank water."

"And you all had some of everything? And you're sure that's all you had?"

Miss FitzEustace nodded twice.

"What," demanded Linnaeus, looking acute, "about bread and condiments?"

"Don't be absurd, Linnaeus," said Lucy. "It's all these detective stories he reads, Miss FitzEustace, where they make such a lot out of trifles."

She was beginning to feel that all this airy discussion of the tragedy was hardly proper. Even though none of them had known Lady Madeleine Osmund well, to have her die so suddenly was very sad and shocking.

Linnaeus ought not to go on and on about it. There was, however, no need to apologize to Miss FitzEustace, who was entering wholeheartedly into the spirit of the cross examination.

"Ah, but I'm sure Mr. Bex is right," said Miss FitzEustace. "It's the little things in life that count. Well, now, let's see. We each had a slice of bread off the same loaf. There were two lots of salt and pepper, one between me and Mr. Osmund, and one between Lady Madeleine and Lord Barna. All the sugar for the sweet came out of the same sifter."

"One of those ration savers that you shake and shake and the sugar won't come out?"

"Yes, one of those. And we all had cream out of the one jug. And there," said Miss FitzEustace, "I think I've told you everything."

"You said potato salad, didn't you? Was that just potato, or were there other things in it?"

"Oh, Mr. Bex, you're very thorough! It was sliced-up potato piled on top of lettuce, with those little raw onions you pull up as thinnings. There wasn't any dressing on it. They passed round some in a jar with a maker's label on. Oh, but talking of salad, wait now a minute!" exclaimed Miss FitzEustace. "Did I mention the horseradish? There was raw grated horseradish round the beef."

"Aha!" said Linnaeus, putting his finger tips together. Lucy resisted a strong temptation to throw something at him.

"It wouldn't be the first time," Linnaeus informed them, "that poisonous roots have been mistaken for horseradish. *Aconitum*, for instance, the genus we were discussing the other afternoon."

"Really?" said Miss FitzEustace. "How odd if—but of course it couldn't have been. Do you know, I always thought till last Saturday that aconites were those little yellow things."

"Oh, you mean *Eranthis.*"

Lucy explained. "You know what gardeners are, Miss FitzEustace. When Linnaeus says *Syringa* he means lilac, and when he means syringa, he calls it *Philadelphus.*"

"Well, I bet you the horseradish was *Aconitum,*" said Linnaeus. Lucy began to look worried, but Miss FitzEustace was greatly relieved.

"Well, I never have cared for those sharp things that give you a red nose," she declared, looking at Linnaeus with a flushed face, over the remains of her apple drink. "I pushed all mine under a lettuce leaf. I don't know what Lord Barna and Mr. Osmund did. Perhaps they didn't have any."

"Perhaps some of it was all right," suggested Linnaeus, "though, in that case, one would expect them to have noticed the difference."

"But wouldn't you expect the cook to have noticed? That's the modern servant for you," said Miss FitzEustace with disgust. "Why, the woman's practically a murderess!"

"She'll probably catch it at the inquest," said Linnaeus.

"Yes, I suppose everything will be cleared up at the inquest," said Lucy, still looking thoughtful.

Mention of the inquest had a depressing effect on Miss FitzEustace. "I've never been mixed up in such a thing in my life," she moaned. "Whatever shall I do if they make me be a witness?"

"Get in touch with your solicitor, Miss FitzEustace," advised Linnaeus.

But Miss FitzEustace's idea of solicitors was that if you gave them the slightest encouragement they would write to you twice a day and charge six and eight a letter. She did not think she required legal advice. What would be a help, if she had to go through such a sordid business, was the support of another woman.

"I was wondering if Miss Bex—?" she ventured diffidently. "I've no right to ask you, but you've been so sympathetic. Would you ever come with me and hold my hand?"

"Lucy likes a bit of life," said Linnaeus heartily.

Lucy did not at all like the idea of intruding on such an occasion. But Miss FitzEustace did not seem to know anybody else in the neighborhood whom she could ask to accompany her and was extremely loath to go alone. So in the end Lucy consented, provided she could keep in the background. Privately she hoped that, after all, Miss FitzEustace's evidence would not be required. So, reluctantly, she promised, and that was how, in spite of herself, she first got drawn into the investigation of the mystery. For the inquest opened up what was soon being called "the Clonmeen mystery," though even after the inquest it was not immediately labeled "murder."

Miss FitzEustace thanked her warmly, drained her glass and stood up to go. "You've taken a weight off my mind," she said. "What a shocking business it is! I don't know how I'm going to break it to Miss Milfoyle. Not, of course, that they were friends, but she's so softhearted, poor thing. Poor Mr. Osmund! You know, I shouldn't wonder if he mightn't like to have the picture finished after all. I could use photographs, you know, and it would be carrying out the last wishes of the deceased. I shall have to call, anyway, for my easel. Not too soon, of course, but it would be a pity to let too many days go by because of the weather. Perhaps after the funeral—" Neither of the Bexes expressed an opinion, so she tailed off into thanks and good-byes, and departed all agog to horrify old Miss Milfoyle.

"That apple wine is rather strong," observed Lucy, clearing away the glasses. "I hope Miss Milfoyle won't think she dropped in at the corner pub. Though who could blame her under the circumstances? What are you looking for, Lin?"

Her brother was going through the living-room bookshelves. The books there were a miscellaneous collection, the leavings of childhood, education, travel and visitors, which none of the family treasured enough to corner for their own rooms. They were shuffled regularly once a year at the spring cleaning, and the resulting unexpectedness of arrangement rather pleased the Bexes. Linnaeus's eye wandered past *Chamonix and Mont Blanc,* Motley's *Dutch Republic, Chess Problems and Stratagems, The Irish Church Hymnal, The Gorilla Hunters, Domestic Cookery by a Lady, Loudon's Encyclopaedia of Gardening, Materia Medica.* He said indignantly, "You've been having another waste paper purge!"

"Not for months," said Lucy. "Not since I sent the old photo albums."

"There used to be a book here called *Poisonous Plants.*"

"You gave it away yourself," said Lucy triumphantly, "to Mrs. McGoldrick's 'Bring a Book and Buy a Book' in aid of the G.F.S. I told you it was a silly one to give, but it was the only thing you would part with."

"Doesn't that just go to show," said Linnaeus, "how you can't safely give away anything, because you're sure to want it?'

"I'm sure nobody bought it. It's probably still at the McGoldricks'."

"I shall ask them. Unless, perhaps, there's something in this." He took down *Materia Medica* and blew the dust off it: "Here we are. Remember Miss Thing said that Lady Madeleine complained of tingling all over? That does suggest aconitine. Listen! 'The first symptom of poisoning is the characteristic tingling which is diagnostic of every variety and preparation of aconite.' And farther back it says monkshood has been mistaken for horseradish."

"So that's that," said Lucy. "And that makes the third time."

"How do you mean?"

"The third time monkshood has cropped up in the last few days. Oh,

I know it might be just coincidence, like reading an odd name in a book and meeting somebody called that next day. But when it ends in a death— it's enough to make one superstitious."

"Evidently," said Linnaeus dryly.

CHAPTER VI
Inquest

AS GENERALLY happens with vague engagements that one makes out of civility, in the hope of not having to keep them, there was no getting out of the inquest, and it was held at a very inconvenient time. Miss FitzEustace telephoned that afternoon to say that it was to be in the schoolhouse at nine next morning (this being school holidays), and would Lucy meet her in the Main Street at ten to? Lucy had to go out leaving bedrooms undone behind her, and with dinner still on her mind. But she was not one to fail in a promise, and the two ladies arrived punctually together.

The schoolhouse, an old-fashioned building with an ecclesiastical touch about its doors and windows, seemed quite an appropriate place for such solemnities, though there were inconveniences about the seating accommodation. A chair and a table for the Coroner were placed on the teacher's dais, and his Clerk had a larger table on the floor in front, but for everybody else there were only desk benches designed for under fourteens. Two rows of these were turned sideways for the jury.

The two ladies sat down modestly at the bottom of the class, and Lucy went on thinking about dinner, while exchanging occasional comments with Miss FitzEustace, who looked round her with curiosity. There were only a handful of people present. Inquests are theoretically open to the public, but as the time and place are only made known to those directly concerned, few casual onlookers are likely to turn up.

Lucy was relieved to see that neither Mr. Osmund nor Lord Barna had yet arrived. If life had been in one of its cross-grained phases, she would have run into them on the threshold. There were two women whom she identified as maids from Annalee Hall; she remembered the housemaid because of her sanctimonious expression, which might have passed for mourning if she had not looked just the same the day that Lucy paid her formal call at the house. The girl with her was younger and flightier, and not too tearful to cast an eye at a young fellow in his best blues, who leaned against the wall opposite. Lucy recognized him by a general family likeness to the Quins at Beechfield and remembered that Larry Quin and the Osmunds' cook were walking out.

She shared these observations with Miss FitzEustace, and Miss FitzEustace in her turn indicated a youth with a notebook, and whispered, "The Press!" Neither of them could place a man in a brown town suit, or a man who wore loose tweeds with a precise expression; these two sat on top of their desks and had an air of being old hands. There were two Civic Guards in uniform. Lucy recognized one of them as the Clonmeen Station Sergeant, whose name was Dunphy; Miss FitzEustace said the other was the Guard who had spoken to her at the Hall. The Station Sergeant, who had made the arrangements, was fiddling with a card on which the words of the oath were printed in large letters; as there was no proper witness box he did not quite know where to put it.

The Coroner's Clerk selected a paper from the heap on his table and called over the names of the jury. "Only nine," whispered Miss FitzEustace, having expected twelve. Lucy did not know any of the jury, and wondered where they had been collected. They all looked curiously alike, and she felt that an up-to-date producer would have put them all into masks.

At ten past nine there was a stir at the door caused by more important arrivals, and in came Mr. Osmund and Lord Barna. They had with them their solicitor and the doctor who had been called in to Lady Madeleine. Another doctor followed, who was the State Pathologist. Immediately afterwards, the Coroner made his entrance. As a matter of fact they had all come down together in his car.

Everybody rose when the Coroner appeared, and Lucy and Miss FitzEustace had to extricate themselves from their desks more suddenly than they had bargained for. Apart from this ceremony there was little formality. Lucy, who had vaguely expected some parade of the majesty of the law, was impressed by the plain and businesslike nature of the proceedings and was glad to feel it must make things easier for the deceased's relatives:

The Coroner began by introducing to the jury the solicitor, Mr. Darcy, who represented the relatives, and the man in the brown town suit, Mr. McInerney, who, surprisingly enough, was another solicitor, representing James Dunne, grocer, of Main Street, Clonmeen; the same grocer with whose wife Lady Madeleine had cashed the postdated check.

Otway Osmund was then called as the first witness. "The poor man, he looks stricken!" breathed Miss FitzEustace in Lucy's ear. To Lucy, he looked very much as usual: his face was inexpressive, and his bearing self-controlled. All that was required of him was to identify the body. Standing by the Clerk's table, he muttered over the words of the oath, which the Clerk held out to him. The Clerk then read aloud the deposition he had already made, giving formal evidence of identification, Osmund swore to it, signed it, and was allowed to sit down again.

Next came the medical evidence, which the doctors read aloud from their own written statements. The man whom the Osmunds had called in was a stranger, not the doctor who practiced in Clonmeen. Sunday afternoon before a bank holiday is an unfortunate time to be taken ill. The Clonmeen doctor had gone away for the weekend, and four others were telephoned to in vain before a message got through to this Dr. Brett. Even then, it was a case of telephoning through to his golf club, whither he had gone on a bicycle, his petrol ration being restricted to professional uses. It was not till after four o'clock that the family had recognized the necessity of calling a doctor in, and the further delays added up to an hour and a half. Had Dr. Brett reached the patient sooner he might have saved her, but he arrived only in time for the final collapse.

All this came out at a later stage. What the doctor read was a description of the patient's symptoms, and this was followed up by the State Pathologist, with an account of the findings of a postmortem which he had performed on the Monday.

Lucy was medical minded enough to listen closely to all the details, and forgot everything else in the interest of learning just how far Lady Madeleine's symptoms corresponded to the description in Linnaeus's text book, *Materia Medica.* But she was recalled to externals by the heavy breathing of Miss FitzEustace at her side, and when she looked at her she found her unfortunate companion had turned pale green. She really seemed to be, as she had anticipated, in need of the services of "another woman." Lucy's method of womanly support and sympathy was to push the sufferer's head well down between her knees (the desk was in the way, but she edged her to the end of the bench). She held Miss FitzEustace down with one hand, and continued to listen with interest while the doctors clearly established that Lady Madeleine had taken a fatal dose of aconitine three or four hours before her death, and (from fragments found in the remains and the excreta) that she had taken it in the form of an uncooked root. Both doctors were then allowed to leave the court, and Lucy permitted Miss FitzEustace to come to the surface.

The next witness was the Clonmeen Station Sergeant, whose mellifluous western brogue was a refreshing change after so many flat Dublin voices. Sergeant Dunphy told how the case of poisoning had been reported to him by the doctor at half-past seven on Sunday evening, and he had at once gone up to the house and secured the remains of the deceased's last meal. He had then telephoned to the Detective Branch at Dublin Castle and asked for a detective to take over the investigation. It was too late to do any more that night, but Detective Inspector Lancey had come down first thing on Monday morning.

Inspector Lancey, whom Miss FitzEustace had ignorantly taken for a mere Guard, now began to take a lead. Sergeant Dunphy had handed over to him the remains of lunch: the cold beef, the sad potatoes, the wilting lettuce, the stale bread, the gooseberries, and of course the horseradish. They had all been sent to the Technical Bureau at Kilmainham for analysis. The analyst's report said that, mixed with fragments of genuine horseradish, they had found a small quantity of grated root of *Aconitum*.

"Commonly called monkshood?" asked the Coroner, for the benefit of the jury. The Inspector confirmed this.

He went on to say that he had been round the garden at Annalee Hall and had found monkshood growing there, but no horseradish. Evidence was going to be offered later that the horseradish was sent round by a shop. "So that," thought Lucy, "is where Dunne comes in."

But now it was time for Miss FitzEustace to perform her public duty, and it was a pity that Lucy's ministrations had pushed her hat well over one eye. It was a wastepaper basket hat, trimmed with raffia, and should have been worn straight, if at all. Looking disheveled but determined, the artist made her way to the table.

The Clerk read aloud her name, with her home address in Dublin and her temporary address at Miss Milfoyle's, and that she was a painter by profession. Lucy saw the young reporter taking particular note and hoped that Miss FitzEustace was going to find a little free publicity some compensation for her ordeal.

Proceeding with Miss FitzEustace's deposition, in a considerably boiled-down version, the Clerk read that she had spent the morning painting Lady Madeleine in the garden and had been with her continuously till lunch time, during which time she had not seen her eat anything; that she had stayed for lunch, had felt no ill effects from the meal, but had not eaten any horseradish; that Lady Madeleine had begun to feel ill about half-past two, and that she had then left. Miss FitzEustace listened with a frown of concentration, started and blinked when the Clerk handed her the page and his pen, and signed with the legible flourish which figured prominently on all her pictures. It was all over within five minutes.

The Clerk then called Lord Barna, prefacing his title with his full name: Roland Denis Marianne Silke. Lucy was charmed by the "Marianne," guessing that his French mother had followed an old custom and given him her own Christian name. Rank eclipsed art in the reporter's notebook. The files would have photographs of his lordship in ballet costume—headline: "DANCING PEER BEREAVED?"—the subeditor could decide whether it was in good taste. To the reporter, Lord Barna looked dissipated and heavy-eyed. To Lucy, he just looked miserable. He showed less self-control than Mr. Osmund and was disturbingly fidgety. But, once on his feet, he seemed to pull himself together. He was the only witness to read the oath audibly, with an attention to punctuation and emphasis that delayed proceedings and tried the patience of the officials. Then he listened gravely, and standing quite still, while the Clerk read unemotionally through his account of the tragic afternoon.

Lord Barna's deposition began a little before the point where Miss FitzEustace's left off. He had gone out about ten and stayed away all morning, only returning for lunch after the others had started. At lunch, he had eaten some horseradish which might have had monkshood mixed with it, as he had suffered from tingling lips and tongue and had felt rather sick, but had said nothing about it in the general upset.

It was he who told of the delay in fetching a doctor. At first they had hesitated to call one in, partly because the patient, like many sick people, had an unreasonable aversion to being treated, and partly because the petrol restrictions made one think twice about bringing a man out from Dublin on what might turn out to be only a slight pretext. Later, when Lady Madeleine became worse, Otway Osmund rang up four doctors in vain and had given up in despair when Lord Barna finally got a message through to Dr. Brett.

Lucy was left with a distressing impression of masculine helplessness in face of illness and told herself that she would have sent for a doctor at once, whatever the patient said, or given an emetic, for anyone with any sense would have seen it to be a case of poisoning. Lord Barna, no doubt, was too young to have much experience of illness, but surely

Mr. Osmund could have done something. He did seem rather a negative person when you met him in company with his self-assertive wife, but he must have capacity of some sort to have reached the position he held in the business world. Probably his distress had made him lose his head. Lucy wondered who had done the necessary nursing. She supposed it must have been the maids, neither of whom looked the sort to rise to an emergency.

Mr. Osmund was at the table again; the Clerk had recalled him to ask if he had eaten any of the horseradish. He replied that he had not, as he did not care for it.

The foregoing evidence did not leave much doubt about the immediate cause of death. The question now was, how had the monkshood got there? The Clerk called the cook, Theresa Glorney.

Theresa had nothing to offer on the subject beyond a wide-eyed stare. Her code was that, when anything untoward came to light, like a breakage in the china cupboard or poison on the dinner table, you knew nothing about it and nobody could put the blame on you.

She did say for herself, however, that she had sent the same horseradish up on Saturday and it had been all right. Not being a girl to give herself two jobs where one would do, she had grated up all the roots on Saturday afternoon, made half into sauce to serve with the hot joint, and set aside the rest to garnish the cold meat next day. Everybody had eaten the sauce at dinner, and nobody had come to any harm.

But the chief point contributed by Theresa was that the horseradish had not been grown in the Hall garden, but was sent up from Dunne's. This naturally brought Mr. McInerney (the brown-suited solicitor) to his feet. He obtained leave from the Coroner to ask the witness a question.

"Now, miss, can you swear that the roots you sent up grated to table were the very same as those sent from the shop ?"

"Yes," faltered Miss Glorney.

"You took them from the boy yourself?"

"Yes, I did."

"But most of the other vegetables for table are grown in the garden?"

"Yes."

"Wouldn't it be very easy, now, for some monkshood roots to have got mixed up with them?"

"I couldn't say."

"Is it you pulls the vegetables?"

"I do not, sir. I get what I want from Larry Quin." Theresa threw a helpless and appealing look at her young man. Larry Quin stepped forward without waiting to be called, but, ignoring him, Inspector Lancey informed the Coroner that there was some other evidence to be offered on that point by the housemaid, Norah Nagle. There was no appeal in the look Theresa gave Norah, and Norah gave her a cold one back. Before the inwardness of this coolness came out, however, there was a digression. One of the jurymen, who had an inquiring mind, wanted to know what had become of the rest of the horseradish sauce from Saturday.

Theresa said she threw it out and further explained that "out" meant into the pig pail, the contents of which were collected at night by the butcher's boy for his uncle's pig. The juryman asked anxiously after the pig. The Detective Inspector had not neglected to follow up this line of inquiry. The contents of the pig pail had been mixed with other scraps from Annalee House and Annalee Lodge, so that it was hopeless to extricate the horseradish, and the butcher's boy's uncle was in two minds whether to throw away the lot or risk it.

The Coroner remarked that, as some of the horseradish was known to have been genuine and harmless, and as nobody had been ill after eating it on Saturday, the fate of the pig was unlikely to have any bearing on the case. Lucy sensed in his manner a blend of approval for a juryman's using his intelligence and disapproval of his wasting time. The juryman sat down.

Theresa Glorney wriggled back into her desk, and Norah Nagle exhumed herself out of hers and advanced with the flat-footed step and firm breathing of one with nothing to hide. Nobody guessed what an amount of trouble the Inspector had had to get a deposition out of her. What she revealed was that the grated horseradish had spent some time on the garden rubbish heap.

When Theresa went to make the sauce she could not find the horseradish which she had grated up a few minutes earlier. Norah told her she must have thrown it out along with an apronful of pea pods. Theresa said she had not, but Norah went to look, and brought back some fragments which she declared on her oath were unmistakably horseradish and not in the least like monkshood.

Dunne's solicitor jumped up at once and asked her if she knew what monkshood looked like. The witness replied that she had been shown a specimen by the Guard (like Miss FitzEustace, she was indifferent to police ranks) and it was quite different. And anyway these roots were already grated. Theresa just blew the dust off them and sent them to table.

The solicitor looked skeptical.. It certainly seemed to Lucy, knowing the heedlessness of maids in general, that they had arrived at a possible explanation. But Inspector Lancey did not look altogether satisfied. The Coroner remained impassive.

"Ye can ask Larry there," said Norah, "and he'll tell ye there never was any monkshood near it at all."

"How long," asked the solicitor, "have you been in Mr. Osmund's service?"

The question put Norah on her dignity. "I was five years with her ladyship and Mr. Osmund, but I was fifteen with the old lord, before her ladyship's marriage." She spoke wistfully. Lucy guessed that her idea of heaven would have been something like the hymn, "forever with the Lord."

The solicitor went on, "That is, you were with the family since before they came to Clonmeen. And since you came here, all the groceries were got at Dunne's?"

"Yes, sir."

"And you often had horseradish?"

"There's many does have it regular now, when ye can't get mustard."

"And you never had any complaint against Dunne's?"

"No, sir."

"Quiet, please!" broke in the Coroner's Clerk. "Quiet! What's the matter there?" A conversation had broken out in the body of the Court between Larry Quin and Theresa. He was talking to her in urgent tones, while she wriggled and looked bashful. But at this sudden attack from on high she plucked up courage to call out,

"Yes, we did have a complaint. There was the bit of glass."

Mr. McInerney looked annoyed at the interruption. In trying to do things handsomely by his client he had overreached himself. He suggested, with a virtuous glance at the Coroner, that whatever Miss Glorney referred to, it was hardly relevant.

"What does she refer to?" asked the Coroner. "Has it anything to do with the case?"

"I don't know, sir," piped Theresa. "It was one time when Norah found a piece of glass in the sugar ration. Mr. Dunne give us an extra two pounds, so we said no more about it."

On this being referred to Norah, she confirmed it sulkily. The Clerk scribbled an addition to her deposition. The solicitor sat down looking disgusted. Nobody had any more questions for Norah, so she was dismissed, and they came at last to Larry Quin.

Larry had been containing himself with difficulty. He was the type of Irishman whose hair naturally stands on end and who looks pugnacious even when he is only mildly exasperated.

"Look at," said Larry, after they had interrupted him once to administer the oath, "what I have to say is, that monkshood never came out of Annalee Hall. Nothing went into or came out of that garden without I'd know it, and I've dug no monkshood, nor there's been no digging near the monkshood, since ever I was in it at all."

"Has the rubbish heap been examined?" asked the Coroner.

"It has, sir," replied the Inspector wearily. "I went over it myself on Monday morning, after talking with the last witness. I found no trace of monkshood, horseradish, or any root vegetable."

"Nor you wouldn't," said Larry. "It isn't the rubbish heap he means at all, sir. It's the compost heap. Where we put the green refuse."

"Oh, indeed," said the Coroner. "You'd better tell the jury what a compost heap is. Some of them may not be gardeners." There was a slight titter, instantly quelled by the Coroner's eye, that disclaimed any intention of joking on serious subjects.

Larry plunged into an explanation of the distinction between a rubbish heap, where things like woody stalks, scutch, and old roots are left to burn, and a compost heap, where vegetable matter is scientifically rotted down with chemicals to make useful manure. Compost is not a new idea, but since the scarcity of manure in the emergency, it had been in the news. There are various methods of making it. The Bexes had done it their own way successfully for years, but Lucy was not above picking up hints from one of a gardening tribe like the Quins. Her attention was distracted, however, by Miss FitzEustace, who nudged her and whispered,

"Do you deal at Dunne's?"

"I do," Lucy whispered back. "I'm registered there for everything."

"Awkward changing one's grocer nowadays."

"Oh, but I shouldn't think of it. I'm sure there's some mistake."

"I wonder does Miss Milfoyle deal there? P'raps I'd better not say anything to unsettle her."

"Much better not," said Lucy, but she reflected that word was sure to go round.

Dunne's solicitor also looked uneasy. He had not managed things very well for his clients. He pressed Larry in vain but could not make him admit that there was any chance of any kind of roots having been thrown on the compost heap. At last the Coroner intervened, dismissed Larry, and glanced inquiringly at the Inspector.

But the Inspector was not letting them off anything. He had still one more witness, the man in homespun tweeds who had been sitting with Mr. McInerney and whom Lucy had not been able to place. He turned out to be an expert. He stood up where he was, just in front of the table, and made the Coroner a little bow. Then he took off his rimless glasses, put them on again to read the oath, took them off again to polish them, and, still polishing, embarked on a little talk on vegetable poisons.

The expert began by saying that he had followed the inquiry with the greatest interest and that he was glad to have been present, because it really was a quite unusual case. He beamed at Mr. Osmund, as at a promising pupil who has raised a good point in class, but something in Osmund's manner may have struck him, for he cleared his throat and addressed his further remarks to the corner of the ceiling.

The most remarkable feature of the case, to the expert, was that the monkshood should have caused death. It was, of course, a well-known poisonous plant, and the root was the most poisonous part. He would certainly not advise anyone to eat any part of the plant, as it would make them very ill. But from the small amount eaten in the case under discussion, he would not have expected fatal consequences. In the textbook case of John Crumpler, a weaver, in Spitalfields, who ate Aconitum by mistake for celery, the doctor did not reach him for some hours, but the patient was treated and recovered. He need not enumerate all the cases where a similar mistake had occurred. There really ought not to be any danger of confusion. Monkshood root is brown outside, whereas horseradish is whitish, and the monkshood when scraped has a distinctive odor. The odor might, of course, pass unnoticed, as many people had a deficient sense of smell, and he fancied that Miss Glorney, for instance, suffered from adenoids. Here the expert cleared his throat again, conscious that he had let himself run on.

There was a very interesting point, he said, in the evidence about the portion of horseradish served as sauce on Saturday. Cooking, that is, boiling, would do away with the poisonous properties, and even if *Aconitum* had been mixed with the first lot of horseradish as well as the second, it would quite probably not produce any ill effects if served in that form. It was even possible that more than one dish of it had been eaten in Clonmeen over the weekend, if, as had been suggested, the roots originated in a local shop. (Mr. McInerney looked as if he considered his neighbor a snake in the grass.) That, however, said the expert, they would never know. But, as he had said before, our garden monkshood was not one of the most poisonous of the species. It was curious that the poisonous properties decreased as you went farther north. In Norway, people actually ate the young shoots as a green vegetable. The poisonous properties also tended to be weakened by cultivation. In England, since the war, they were cultivating *Aconitum Napellus* for the drug trade, but in normal times the manufacturers preferred to import it from Germany where it grew wild. Not that *Napellus* was the deadliest of the family. There was a highly poisonous kind which contained nepaline as well as aconitine, and was less used in manufacture. He referred to *Aconitum ferox*.

"What's the matter?" asked Miss FitzEustace in Lucy's ear.

"Didn't you hear—?" But one more Latin name meant nothing to Miss FitzEustace. "Nothing," said Lucy hastily. "Hasn't it got very hot in here?"

"Shall we try and get someone to open a window?"

"Not worth it, they've nearly finished."

"Thank goodness. I thought that man would never stop."

But the expert had run down at last, and the Coroner's Clerk, who had taken down the gist of his remarks in longhand, finally caught up with him. The expert glanced through the abridged version of his lecture and signed it, and Inspector Lancey said to the Coroner,

"That's all the evidence now."

The Coroner asked if either of the solicitors had anything to say to the jury. The Osmunds' solicitor preserved the weighty silence that had enveloped him throughout. The brown-suited solicitor made a last effort for his client, by referring the jury again to the evidence about the roots having been left out in the garden. Whether or not they split hairs about the difference between a rubbish heap and a compost heap, the point remained that the roots had been lying about among other garden stuff where a substitution could easily have occurred.

The Coroner then told the jury the whole story again from the beginning. He said there would not be much doubt in their minds about the immediate cause of death, but on the further point of how the poison came there, they might not be quite clear. They had heard that roots which should have been horseradish, but some of which might have been monkshood, had been sent to the house from a shop. They had also heard that those roots had been thrown out in the garden, where monkshood was actually growing, and lay there for a quarter of an hour or more, during which time they might have got mixed up with other vegetable matter. Against that they had to consider the statement of Lawrence Quin, that no monkshood roots were anywhere near the part of the garden where these roots were thrown out, and the statement of the Inspector, that neither monkshood roots nor horseradish roots had been found there since. If a substitution took place on the compost heap, it seemed likely that some monkshood roots would have remained there, but they might have been scattered by the wind, or by rats or other creatures; before the Inspector arrived. They must certainly bear in mind the distinction between a rubbish heap and a compost heap, and the unlikelihood of any kind of roots being found on the latter. The fact that the horseradish roots were already grated would tend to make confusion with other roots less likely. If the jury came to the conclusion that the substitution did not occur in the garden, they would then ask themselves whether there was any evidence that monkshood roots were sent by mistake from the shop, and if it seemed to them that there was an open chance whether the mistake occurred there or somewhere else, they must make this clear in their verdict, leaving the matter open for further inquiries.

With these clear directions for their guidance the jury went out, and everyone else relaxed in their various ways, some whispering, some coughing, some crossing or uncrossing their legs. The Coroner began to write something and, so to speak, took his eye off the class. The two Guards and the Coroner's Clerk conducted a secular conversation in religious undertones. Mr. McInerney started a whispered argument with the expert. The reporter doodled on a blank page. Lord Barna fidgeted with his signet ring. Mr. Osmund talked business with his solicitor. Miss FitzEustace sighed, hoped they would not be long, was glad she had not got to make up her mind about it all and wondered what Miss Bex was thinking. But Lucy kept her thoughts to herself; she was saving them up for Mrs. Nichol-Jervis.

After about ten minutes, or the time it had taken all of them to smoke cigarettes, the jury came back, and their foreman handed the Coroner a written statement. The Coroner read aloud the verdict that,

1. The death was due in accordance with the medical evidence.

2. There was no evidence to show where the monkshood had come from.

There was a long pause while the Clerk, the solicitors, and the reporter wrote this down (Lucy thought of the guinea pigs in *Alice in Wonderland* and their squeaky slate pencils). Then the Coroner announced his finding in accordance with the verdict, ending up informally with,

"That's all now."

And the Court was dismissed.

CHAPTER VII
Aconitum Ferox

MISS Fitz-Eustace thanked Lucky warmly for coming, and they parted in the Main Street. Lucy had her August soap coupons to cash, so she turned automatically into Dunne's. She found Mrs. Dunne alone in the shop, having a real good cry.

"Why, Mrs. Dunne!" exclaimed Lucy. She had known the Dunnes all her life and felt too old a friend to be embarrassed. Mrs. Dunne looked up at her and sobbed,

"Oh, Miss Bex, isn't it terrible about her ladyship?"

"Yes, indeed," said Lucy.

"Terrible," repeated Mrs. Dunne. "If it was the blackest stranger you'd pity them. But sure, you, Miss Bex, won't believe what they're all saying now."

"What do you mean?" asked Lucy, though of course she guessed.

Mrs. Dunne swallowed down another sob. "There's some saying that it was something she got from this shop."

Lucy said firmly, "Nonsense!" Where comfort was needed she saw no sense in half measures.

"You've dealt with us for years," said Mrs. Dunne, "and Mrs. Bex, God rest her! before you, and we never sent you anything but the best of quality."

"Of course you haven't," said Lucy. "And I shall say so, Mrs. Dunne, if ever I hear the subject mentioned."

Mrs. Dunne looked somewhat cheered. "James and me's always been so careful," she declared, gazing at Lucy earnestly. "We couldn't bear to think of a thing like that happening. We could never hold up our heads again in Clonmeen. You don't know how hard it is, Miss Bex, nowadays especially, to keep up the quality and be sure things are wholesome, with substitutes for this and substitutes for that, and everything coming loose in bags instead of done up in packets. But as for the vedges, sure we never have any but what we grow in our own garden. It's just a sideline, like. Miss Bex, if you'd step through here a minute, I'll show you the very place where we dig the horseradish."

Lucy, who felt very sorry for the woman, could not refuse. She was ushered through a short, dark passage into a small but wildly luxuriant kitchen garden, where rank rhubarb crowded monster marrows into a tangle of unthinned raspberry canes, while scarlet runners leapt up into an apple tree which scattered its windfalls over the lot. The horseradish had made one corner its own, smothering everything else with its large tropical-looking leaves. Profusion and confusion reigned together. But though Lucy looked everywhere, she could not see any monkshood.

She did not, in any case, think the monkshood had come from there, and she assured Mrs. Dunne of that, with real sincerity and sympathy. Mrs. Dunne, the decent old soul, was worrying only over the imputation of responsibility for the tragedy, but Lucy saw most clearly the damaging effect the rumor might have on the little business which James Dunne and his wife had built up over so many years. She was confirmed in a resolution she had taken at the inquest: to go and talk to Mrs. Nichol-Jervis about the stolen *Aconitum ferox*.

The first thing, however, was to get back to Annalee Lodge, where her old Lizzie was waiting for guidance. Lucy having, in the midst of her preoccupations, managed by this time to think out dinner, instructed Lizzie to mince the last remains of the joint, and to make a batter, and she, Lucy, would unite the two into meat pancakes later. She then did her midday tour of the garden with a watering-can and gathered up a cauliflower and some stewing plums to complete the meal. Old Lizzie announced that she had done the bedrooms, which were Lucy's job. Lucy suspected that meant she probably had not swept down the basement stairs and passage, but thanked her and forbore to investigate. Luckily, dusting could be scamped for a day, out here in the clean country air. So that settled the chores, and Lucy sat down in peace to a bread and cheese lunch.

It seemed best to go to Beechfield immediately after lunch and not encroach again so soon on the Nichol-Jervises' rations by dropping in to tea. So without letting herself be tempted into a siesta, Lucy put on anti-glare glasses and faced the dusty walk. The novelty of the fine weather was wearing off by now, while the heat had increased. The macadam road was sticky and reeked not of petrol but horse droppings. There was shade in the avenue, but also flies, and here stones slipped underfoot and the dust powdered Lucy's shoes. She was thankful to come out on the lawn in front of the house, where she found Mrs. Nichol-Jervis on a swung seat under an awning, under the protection of the mightiest of all the beech trees.

"I am too hot to sit beside anybody," said Lucy, as Mrs. Nichol-Jervis put her feet down and invited her to share the seat. She took a cushion and sat on the grass and gladly accepted a cigarette. "It does seem ungrateful when we get so little fine weather, but I really do wish it would rain again."

"The heat is very trying," said Mrs. Nichol-Jervis, with such emphasis that Lucy guessed it was not only the heat. "Ernest professes to enjoy it, but it does not suit me at all. Ernest has gone into Dublin, and Wendy is out for a walk with Lord Barna."

"It is you I have come to see," said Lucy, wondering whether she had imagined a special inflection in her friend's familiar tones. "At least," she corrected herself, "it's a matter for Ernest too, but I will start on you. Isn't this a dreadful business about poor Lady Madeleine? I suppose you know what happened?"

"Oh yes, indeed, we have heard all about it," declared Mrs. Nichol-Jervis, not at all in the appropriate voice of regret, but with something much more like exasperation. Lucy was put out of her stride.

"Well, that saves a lot of explanation," she said. "The real reason I came was on account of Mrs. Dunne."

"Mrs. Dunne?"

"Yes, Mrs. Dunne at the shop. Perhaps you hadn't heard that part of the story." Lucy explained how the Dunnes were involved. "So I wondered," she ended, "do the police know about the monkshood that was stolen from you?"

Mrs. Nichol-Jervis was vague. "I daresay Ernest mentioned it. Of course it was the figs he was really annoyed about."

"But did they pay attention? And do you think they realized it was an extra poisonous variety?"

"I don't know. Does it matter?"

"Of course it matters," said Lucy impatiently. "Don't you understand? It may have been your monkshood that poisoned Lady Madeleine!"

"I should say, most unlikely."

"Say what you like. But it was far more poisonous than any other variety to be found in the neighborhood, and it was knocking about somewhere loose on Saturday night."

"That wasn't our fault. I don't see any need for us to get mixed up in it."

"There is no question of your getting mixed up in anything. All you need do is to make sure Ernest has reported the theft of your plant to the police. Let them know it was *Aconitum ferox*, and extra dangerous. You need not say anything about Lady Madeleine. Let them put two and two together."

"It will seem very stupid to report it now."

Lucy began to feel cross. "If you would rather not be bothered," she said sharply, "I hope you won't mind if I go to the Guards myself and tell them that I heard *Aconitum ferox* mentioned at the inquest, and thought it would be in the public interest to report that there was a plant in the district. Why, there may be some more roots about."

"Oh, if you think it's so important—" Mrs. Nichol-Jervis sighed. "I'll talk to Ernest when he comes in. At any rate it will divert his mind. He is seriously worried just now. We both are."

"Are you?" said Lucy. "What about?" Having gained her point she felt more sympathetic. She reached up and patted her friend's hand as it trailed on the seat of the swinging couch. Certainly something more than the heat was the matter with Mrs. Nichol-Jervis. "Have I been just one more thing on top of another?" asked Lucy. "Or can I help?"

"I am not sorry you came," Mrs. Nichol-Jervis conceded. "I could not really talk about it to anyone but you. It is such a comfort to know one can depend on you, Lucy, and though it isn't exactly a secret, you will understand that we don't want to say very much about it just at present. What I am trying to tell you is, Wendy has got herself engaged to Lord Barna."

Quite unprepared to have her mind switched on to such a different topic, Lucy made the wrong comment. She said, "Already?"

Wendy's mother looked reproachful. "I don't know why you should say that. I had no idea of anything between them. Not an inkling."

"Oh, neither had I," Lucy hastily disclaimed. "It was just that, well, he is good-looking, and there isn't anybody else, is there?"

"This wicked war," said Mrs. Nichol-Jervis, chalking up one more account to Hitler. It was not only that the war had drawn away so many young men of the Nichol-Jervises' circle—even without a war there had always been a steady outflow of nice eligible bachelors to the Empire—but the war also prevented the possibility of Wendy's being sent traveling after them. She stayed at home, taking things off her mother's shoulders and getting an excellent training in housekeeping, while they got engaged to English girls who drove lorries and manned guns.

Lucy asked, "When did it happen?"

"My dear, the very day of the accident! Or night, rather. He came round nearly at midnight on Sunday evening. The two of them had made a plan to go to the theater on Monday, and just to show you how little there was between them, they were each paying for themselves, and Wendy was to book the seats. Well, of course, Roland couldn't go. And after all that dreadful business of Lady Madeleine, the last thing he did on that awful night was to come round here and tell Wendy."

"He must have been very much upset. He's so highly strung."

"If only Ernest would consent to have a telephone," said Mrs. Nichol-Jervis bitterly. "Well, my dear, you can imagine what happened. There was the young man in a great state of nerves, and darling Wendy is so sympathetic, and they stayed out in the garden talking for hours, and there was a moon. There would be a moon. It was so late that I was in bed. Wendy came and tapped on my door to see if I was still awake, and when I asked her if she knew what time it was, she hadn't an idea. Then she told me about Lady Madeleine, and, as if that wasn't upsetting enough, next thing she told me that she and Roland were engaged. The rest of that night I just couldn't get any sleep at all."

Lucy thought it was tactless of Wendy not to wait till morning, knowing how her mother hated late hours. That in itself was quite enough to make Mrs. Nichol-Jervis take a poor view of the engagement. When the surprise wore off she would probably reconcile herself to the idea. Meanwhile it would do most good to let her talk herself out. She asked,

"What does Ernest think?"

"Ernest agrees with me that it would never have happened if it hadn't been for this dreadful tragedy. Fortunately Lady Madeleine's death is quite reason enough for not putting it in the paper yet."

"Is it a secret?"

Mrs. Nichol-Jervis instinctively disliked the idea of a secret engagement. "Not exactly," she replied. "But you do understand, don't you, that we're not taking it at all seriously?"

Lucy accepted this understatement at its face value. After a pause she remarked, "Wendy's twenty-five, isn't she? Two years older than Ivor."

"I was thirty when I married."

"I know, I know." Lucy had not exactly known Mrs. Nichol-Jervis's age, but meant that, whatever Jane Austen might have thought, twenty-five could not nowadays be considered late to marry. In Clonmeen it was hardly even grown up. There was, however, this difference in outlook between herself and Wendy's mother: Lucy, as a spinster, thought that, while it was all very well for exceptional women like herself to be independent, the general run of her sex had better marry than burn ("burn" with a ladylike frittering away of energy, not the exciting flame envisaged by Saint Paul); whereas Mrs. Nichol-Jervis imagined that, if she had never been united to her Ernest by the mysterious workings of Providence, rather than marry anybody else, she would have settled down contentedly as the companion of her parents' old age. Moreover, she herself had had five proposals, and though they were all rather ridiculous, she could not help feeling that this was a normal number, and that there was something indecent about accepting one's very first.

"But he's nice," said Lucy. "I really liked him very much, what I saw of him."

"Oh, he can make himself agreeable, I grant you. His manners are all right."

"And Wendy will be a ladyship."

Mrs. Nichol-Jervis only sniffed. "What good will that do her? He is not Wendy's type at all, any more than Lady Madeleine was mine. They are simply not our sort."

"Has he told you anything about himself?"

"Only that he has no money. He was quite frank about that. Two hundred a year of his own, and now some trifling property that Lady Madeleine had a life interest in, but nothing to speak of."

"He has his profession."

"He isn't even qualified yet. He has no business to think of marriage."

Lucy reflected that the Nichol-Jervises could well afford to give their only daughter a dowry that would tide the young couple over the early years before Lord Barna began to make money. She could not see any sensible objection to the match. Her heart warmed to romance, and she meant to foster it all she could. Linnaeus should work on Ernest and together they would bring Wendy's parents round. One part of her mind was already busy choosing wedding presents.

But she knew better than to press the argument too far.

"Well, thank you for letting me know how things stand," she said, getting up. "I won't tell the Miss Cuffes. May I tell Linnaeus, though? You know he has a great opinion of Wendy."

"Oh yes, Lin ought to be told. Are you trying to go? I hoped you had come to tea."

"Not today, thank you. I have jobs to do in the house. I only dropped in to ask you about the *Aconitum*. You won't forget to speak to Ernest?"

"Oh yes," said Mrs. Nichol-Jervis, who had forgotten all about the *Aconitum*.

"Then good-bye. I am so sorry you are so worried. Give my love to Wendy, won't you?"

The two ladies kissed affectionately. Lucy turned again to the dusty, fly-haunted drive. Before she reached the iron gates she passed a Civic Guard going up to the house. She wondered if they were on the same errand.

CHAPTER VIII
Pursuing a Clue

A SHORT ANNOUNCEMENT of Lady Madeleine Osmund's death ("Funeral private. No flowers.") had appeared in Tuesday's *Irish Times*, and she was buried at Mount Jerome on Wednesday morning. That afternoon Lucy met Lord Barna in the Main Street of Clonmeen. It is always hard to know what to say to the recently bereaved, when some allusion to their loss is indispensable, yet any reminder is likely to give pain. In the circumstances, Lucy would have gone out of her way to avoid the meeting, but she came on him quite unexpectedly round a corner. It was outside Noonan's, the butcher's. He turned to her a face of such despair that she could not get out a word, and it was he who spoke first. He said, "They're shut."

"Of course," said Lucy, recovering herself. "It's early closing day."

"Damn!" said Lord Barna. Then there was a pause fraught with embarrassment, till Lucy said with shy formality,

"My brother and I are so very sorry for your sad loss. Will you please express our deep sympathy to poor Mr. Osmund?"

"Thank you," said Lord Barna miserably, and there was another awkward pause, till in desperation Lucy went on, "But there is something else I should like to tell you. I was so very pleased to hear about you and Wendy Nichol-Jervis."

Lord Barna looked greatly taken aback. "Were you, Miss Bex? How kind of you. But who told you?"

"I was at Beechfield yesterday and had a long talk with Wendy's mother. We are very old friends, you know. But I promise you I will not be indiscreet."

"No, no. We don't want it to be a secret really. It's only that this doesn't seem quite the time— As a matter of fact," said Lord Barna confidentially, "I haven't yet been able to tell poor old Otway. It's sort of difficult, you see. And I should hate him to hear of it suddenly from somebody else."

"I do understand. And I don't think you need worry. I should not have been told only that I am a very old friend, and they look on me as safe."

"I know I don't deserve it," said Lord Barna ingenuously. "I can hardly believe my luck."

Lucy smiled. "Well, but I think Wendy is lucky too."

"I think poor Madeleine would have liked it."

"I'm sure she would."

The subject had had the desired cheering effect, so that Lucy ventured to ask, "And poor Mr. Osmund, how is he?"

"Quite well," replied Lord Barna, "but I think he is still rather stunned by all this. He never was a person to open up much—he's an introverted type, of course—and at present there is no getting at him. I thought I had better stay on at the Hall for a bit. It seemed heartless to go away and leave him there alone. But honestly, I don't know whether he wants me."

"I am sure he would miss you if you went. And there must be a lot of business you can help with."

"Oh no, the solicitor is well up to all that. No, there doesn't seem much for me to do except stand by in the evenings. One tries to sort of emanate sympathy. Tomorrow I shall have to go back to the office. I thought unless Otway said anything, I'd make that an excuse to retire to the flat. But the trouble now is, there's a domestic crisis."

"Oh dear," said Lucy, and her expression encouraged him to tell her all about it.

"The cook," said Lord Barna, "got upset by the police. She walked out on us yesterday afternoon."

"The creature!"

"Yes. Luckily Norah, the housemaid, is still there. She's an institution. So she's carrying on—according to her lights."

"And can she manage?"

"Well, I'm not sure. And I can't decide whether I ought to go away and make less work for her, or stay and lend a hand."

"The work can't be very heavy with only two of you. She's quite able-bodied, isn't she?"

"Oh quite. The trouble is, I don't think she's much of an organizer. For instance, I don't quite know what we shall do about tonight's dinner, because there doesn't seem to be anything in the house, and now the shops are shut."

Lucy gazed at him, visualizing the situation of the two benighted men. "Surely she has something in that she could use. Bacon and eggs, for instance, or tinned stuff ?"

"The only tins left seem to be asparagus and anchovies. There were some tins of meat labelled 'a meal for two,' but they turned out to be only a small helping for one. We had the last three for lunch. We had bacon last night, and finished the rest of it this morning. There are two eggs, but we shall want something for breakfast." Lord Barna began to laugh. "I assure you, things are serious."

Lucy could not help laughing too. It caused some scandal among several old Clonmeen worthies who were watching the encounter through their lace curtained upper windows.

"No, but really," said Lucy. "Something must be done about it or you will starve. Let me think." She remembered that on Wednesday afternoon, not only in Clonmeen but also in Dublin all the provision shops would be closed. She mentally ran through the contents of her own larder. "I could send you over some tinned bully beef—" she began. Then there came to her mind the fact that Noonan's had that morning sent her a larger joint than she had ordered, and there would be plenty to spare.

"Look here," she plunged. "Do you think you could bear to come and dine with my brother and me? Come just for the meal, and you need not stay a moment afterwards. Norah could come too, and have hers in the kitchen with my old Lizzie. That would save her all the preparation and washing up. Unless you think it would be too trying for Mr. Osmund?"

But Lord Barna jumped at the idea. "I think it would be the very best thing for him. He is very depressed and shut up in himself, but it doesn't seem to affect his appetite. It really is most kind of you. But shouldn't we be in the way?"

"No, do come. We shan't be grand, you know, but I can at least give you a square meal. You can slip across the back way through the fence; we'll leave the back door to the garden unlocked."

"Thank you ever so much."

"I hope eight o'clock isn't too late for you?" said Lucy, remembering something. "It's generally half-past seven, but this evening when Linnaeus comes home we have to go up to Mrs. McGoldrick's for a Flower Show meeting."

"Last night," said Lord Barna, "we didn't get anything till after nine."

"What a shame!" said Lucy. "Well then, that's settled. But remember, if Mr. Osmund doesn't want to come, you must ring me up and we will think of something else. And I'll tell you what," she went on, now in the full tide of benevolence, "if you liked, I could come over tomorrow morning and have a talk with Norah. I expect I could help her to plan things out."

"That would be awfully, awfully kind of you," exclaimed Lord Barna. "I mean that. I suppose housekeeping doesn't seem so complex to a woman, but it has been rather too much, these last few days. It's—it's such an intrusion! When one has been through a shattering experience one longs to be alone to think it out. Death is something so fundamental—something that has to be integrated in one's personality. And then people keep coming at you to unstop a blocked up waste pipe, or find enough change to pay the laundry!"

"I know, I know," murmured Lucy, as indeed she did. It went to her head rather, to be rescuing a handsome young nobleman in distress. She found herself lightly undertaking to put everything at Annalee Hall to rights. She would come round first thing in the morning and set the house running on oiled wheels. But meanwhile, she must tear herself away, if she was to do her errands and be home in time to prepare old Lizzie for visitors. Dinner would do as it stood, but Lizzie must have due notice of the event or she would be in a fluster.

Lucy's business in the village was to interview the sexton about an urn, not funereal, but tea. She meant to borrow it for the Flower Show and hoped to have the matter settled before the committee meeting that evening. She also meant to take this opportunity to satisfy the private curiosity she felt about the monkshood that had appeared in her altar flower arrangement.

Having secured her urn, she asked for the keys of the church, leaving Duffy to suppose, if he thought about it, that she had left something inside, or intended some private devotions. The monkshood was still there in the left-hand vase. She went up and inspected it closely, and, going on a gardener's clear recollection of the plants at Beechfield, she had no doubt it was *Aconitum ferox*.

Lucy walked thoughtfully back to the sexton's cottage. Professional detectives seem to find it easy to put casual questions and extract relevant answers, but she could not think of any better way of leading up to the subject than a plain inquiry.

"Them flowers?" said Duffy, his fingers caressing the pipe he was longing to put back in his mouth. "You mean, where did they come from? Lessee now, Miss Cuffe was July, but last Sunday was August. Now who's this is August? Would it be Mrs. Atkinson-Roche?"'

"I am August," said Lucy patiently, "but I didn't put in that monkshood."

Duffy did not appear to have noticed the monkshood.

Fortunately, Duffy's eldest daughter, Christina, a child of fifteen who ran both him and the house, had been keeping in touch with the conversation. She came out into the little passage with a half-peeled potato in her hand, to say,

"Is it the blue flowers, Miss Bex? A lady brought them on Sunday morning before early service."

"That's right!" said Duffy helpfully. "She did so. She come in with them in her hand and put them in the vase."

"Didn't she say anything about it?"

"No, miss, not to me. But she was muttering to herself, like."

"How very odd! And you don't know who she was?"

Christina again came to the rescue. "Wasn't it that lady who's staying at Miss Milfoyle's?"

"Really!" said Lucy, much surprised to find her trail lead to Miss FitzEustace. She did think an artist ought to have known better than to poke in the extra spike of the wrong shade of blue among her pastel colored Buddleias and scabiouses. "Muttering to herself" too! There must be more about the woman than met the eye. She would have to think out the best way of approach. Conscious of amateurishness in her present investigation, Lucy jerked herself out of her abstraction and belatedly attempted to efface the impression she must have made on the Duffys by saying carelessly, "Oh, you mean Miss FitzEustace.

Why, I saw her only yesterday, and I could have asked her what I wanted to know. But it doesn't matter; I'm sure to be seeing her again. Then, will you bring the urn up in your handcart on Saturday week? That will be splendid. Thank you so much."

Lucy did not get back to Annalee Lodge in time to save old Lizzie a fluster, for Lord Barna had already been talking to her on the telephone. Lizzie hated the telephone anyway, being rather deaf, and this time the message she had heard was so improbable that she could not believe she had got it right. Lord Barna had said, "Will you tell Miss Bex not to bother about dinner for Norah tonight, as she would rather stay behind and have bread and tea, but that Mr. Osmund and I will both be very glad to come."

When Lucy finally succeeded in convincing her, first, that she, Miss Bex, had invited guests to dinner at four hours' notice, and second, that Mr. Osmund was dining out on the very day that he buried his wife, old Lizzie said in a disapproving voice, "Then I'll be getting out the finger bowls?" and looked more scandalized than ever when Lucy said that she did not think they need bother with finger bowls as it was not a party. Lizzie could not feel that informality mitigated the callousness of the Osmunds. Their behavior was on their own conscience, but if they were coming at all, they ought to be treated as quality.

Exhausted by explanations, Lucy asked for tea and had it in the garden with Remus, the cat. She had just tilted up the last dregs of the pot, when Linnaeus arrived back early from town, having made a special effort on account of the Flower Show meeting. He was rushed and tired and had missed his own tea, so in spite of the serious inroad on the rations, Lucy thought she had better make him a cup for himself before she broke to him the prospect for the evening. She knew he was unlikely to share her enthusiasm for comforting widowers and orphans in their affliction.

Linnaeus did not reproach her. But when he went upstairs to wash and tidy himself for the meeting, Lucy heard him warbling a snatch of Gilbert and Sullivan,

> "The question is, had he not been
>   A thing of beauty,
> Would she be swayed by quite as keen
>   A sense of duty?"

Family life often makes it difficult to indulge one's personal impulses of benevolence.

CHAPTER IX
Committee Meeting

IN OTHER YEARS the Flower Show had been nothing more than a side-show at the annual garden fête of the Protestant church. It was a popular sideshow, attracting more and more entries every year, but the church funds did not get much out of it, as the expense of hiring staging and vases usually cancelled out the entry and admission fees. This year it had been decided to make a break with the fête and its Church of Ireland associations and to launch the show on a more ambitious scale. It was to be held at Annalee House instead of in the front field at the rectory. Some gardening Catholics had come on the Committee, and a subscription list had been opened for founding a Clonmeen Horticultural Society.

Clonmeen's response to the idea had been encouraging. Subscriptions and promises of entries had come in from all sorts of people of varying incomes, religions, and politics, who had a common interest in gardening. Arrangements were now almost complete, with the Clonmeen brass and reed band and the opening ceremony by a T.D. for the final finishing touches. And just at this stage, ten days before the show date, Mrs. McGoldrick's husband threw a spanner into the works.

For Mrs. McGoldrick had a husband. He was away so much that Clonmeen forgot his existence for weeks on end, but he was by no means a cipher.

Mr. McGoldrick owned a tannery, a boot and shoe factory, and five retail shops in different country towns and spent most of his time traveling from one to another in his charcoal-driven van. He had only come home for the bank holiday weekend. It was then that he heard about the latest developments in connection with the Flower Show: Mr. O'Gallchobhair and the band. Instead of being pleased, Mr. McGoldrick declared that this was beyond anything he had conceived of when he agreed to having the show in his grounds. He would not undertake to be civil to anybody of Mr. O'Gallchobhair's politics, nor would he have a band playing *The Soldier's Song* on his premises. Either no band and no T.D. or they must hold the show somewhere else.

Mr. McGoldrick said all this to Mrs. McGoldrick and then went off on another business tour, leaving her to put his objections before the Committee. It was rather hard on Mrs. McGoldrick, but she was a bland, easygoing person, whom nothing troubled much. She felt it was just like George and assumed that the Committee would put up with his peculiarities as resignedly as she did herself. She sent round post cards asking them to come on Wednesday at six. She seated them round her drawing room on pseudo-antique chairs (it was a kind of parody of Mrs. Nichol-Jervis's drawing room). She gave them sherry, made them a cheerily apologetic little speech, and sat back, smiling, to await their solution.

The Committee were: the Bexes and Wendy Nichol-Jervis, Dora Cuffe, Mr. and Mrs. Naylor, a Colonel Murray and a Mr. Lynch. Dora Cuffe was one of the three Miss Cuffes who were proverbial in Clonmeen for gossip; it went with being energetic and good natured and invaluable at getting up anything from theatricals to a first aid post. The Naylors were well-to-do Catholics with daughters of ages to match the McGoldricks' daughters and great believers in young people getting together. Colonel Murray was an elderly Protestant widower, and Mr. Lynch was a young Catholic bachelor. Mr. Lynch was supposed to be a political extremist. After Mrs. McGoldrick had explained her husband's attitude, several people looked nervously at Mr. Lynch, and Mr. Lynch looked down his nose.

At last kindhearted Mrs. Naylor broke the tension by supposing that, after all, they could do without a band.

"Perhaps we could have the wireless," she suggested.

"Oh but the programs nowadays—" cried Miss Cuffe. "So unsuitable, don't you think? So much propaganda, I mean. I mean, don't you think people want to forget the war?"

"Get hold of a gramophone," advised Mr. Naylor. "Easy matter to connect up a loudspeaker and bring it out on the lawn."

"But the band would be so disappointed," said Wendy Nichol-Jervis. "They've been having extra practices specially for us. It would be a shame to go back on them now."

Colonel Murray cleared his throat, as he always did before speaking, to secure attention. "I take it," he said, "that Mr. McGoldrick's objection is not to the band, but to the playing of *The Soldier's Song*. I must say I have some sympathy with him—"

"Oh, but why, Colonel Murray?" interrupted Miss Cuffe, who went in for being broad-minded. "After all, it's a grand tune."

"My objection was not on musical grounds," said the Colonel. "However, I was going to suggest that the band be asked not to play that particular tune on this particular occasion."

"But don't they have to?" asked Mrs. Naylor. "Isn't it the law, or something?"

"Anyway," said Wendy, "there would be a kind of awkwardness about asking them a thing like that. Some of them mightn't like it."

"Exactly," said Miss Cuffe. "They have their principles."

" 'That's so like a band'," murmured Linnaeus, his mind still running on Gilbert and Sullivan.

There was a general silence.

"And what," demanded Miss Cuffe, "are we going to do about Mr. O'Gallchobhair?"

More silence.

"Has he definitely accepted?" asked Mr. Naylor. "Can we put him off?"

Lucy Bex found speech. Mr. O'Gallchobhair was her own idea and pet contribution. It was she who, *per pro.* Linnaeus, had corresponded with the T.D.'s secretary. "Of course he's accepted," she exclaimed. "And it was very good of him because he's a very busy man. He might easily never have answered at all, but his secretary wrote such a nice letter. You can't possibly put him off now."

"If he didn't come, some other people mightn't," said Wendy.

"I do so agree with Miss Bex," said Miss Cuffe, leaning forward earnestly. "What I felt about inviting Mr. O'Gallchobhair was that it was a Gesture, and I do think that, whatever one's private views may be, one should set an example of tolerance. Up to now our work has been done in such a nice broad spirit. Now if we drag in politics, I do feel, don't you, that it would set the whole thing on a lower plane?"

"And mean a falling off in the takings," said Mr. Lynch. "Going to be hard enough to cover expenses."

Wendy said "Hear, hear!" and Mrs. Naylor said "Oh, dear!" but the effect was the same. Colonel Murray asked if he might see the list of subscribers, and Mrs. McGoldrick took it out of a folder and handed it across. Miss Cuffe looked over his shoulder and pointed out names of people who, in her opinion, would not have been supporters but for the prestige of Mr. O'Gallchobhair.

"Let alone the ones who'll come just to get a look at him," added Mrs. Naylor.

Colonel Murray cleared his throat again and everybody waited.

"I propose," he said formally, "that a deputation be sent from this Committee to discuss the matter with Mr. McGoldrick. Possibly when he understands how far the arrangements have gone, he will see fit to modify his objections."

"I'm afraid he won't be back here till Saturday," said Mrs. McGoldrick, "which is leaving it rather late. But I can assure you that he did understand the position, because I argued and argued with him, but I'm afraid I only put his back up. Men can be so pig-headed," said Mrs. McGoldrick, beaming indulgently at the four men present.

"Er, will Mr. McGoldrick be away on the day of the Flower Show?" asked Mr. Lynch.

"I'm afraid we can't count on it," smiled Mrs. McGoldrick.

It did seem a pity.

"Suppose," said Linnaeus Bex, "we consider the problem from another angle. We've all agreed that it wouldn't do to throw over the T.D., and I think we'd all like the band too, so hadn't we better hold the show somewhere else?"

Everybody told him at once that they had been into all that long ago, and there wasn't anywhere. Linnaeus waved them off.

"I know, I know. And I know what I have in mind isn't as grand as having the show here at the McGoldricks'. But though we aren't quite so spacious, I think if we make the most of the tennis court and the stable yard, as well as the small paddock at the back, we ought to be able to fit in everything at Annalee Lodge."

Lucy could hardly believe her ears. Such a suggestion to come from her unsociable brother, who ordinarily devoted his best efforts to defending his peace and privacy. Did he realize what it would mean? Helpers all over the place from early dawn, all of them wanting looking after and some of them wanting meals. Endless kettles to boil. People in and out of the kitchen, borrowing things. Old Lizzie unable to give her mind to anything for a week before and after. The dust, and, if it rained, the mud. The public stealing cuttings and picking flowers. It was all very well for Mrs. McGoldrick, who liked a bustle, and who anyhow had daughters to do all the hard work, but she and Linnaeus would be found at the end of the day, one weeping in the attic and the other in the cellar, as after their first children's party.

All the same, Linnaeus must be really keen on the Flower Show (which he had pretended to patronize solely to oblige her). And it was nice to have this evidence that her brother, who never expressed a political opinion, shared her disapproval of the line taken by Mr. McGoldrick. And it saved her face with Mr. O'Gallchobhair. And his landing her with a whole Flower Show was much worse than her landing him with visitors for dinner, so she need not any longer feel remorseful about that. So Lucy cheered up, and, as everybody else was praising and thanking Linnaeus, she hastened to appropriate a share of the credit.

Mrs. McGoldrick, relieved though disappointed, insisted on more sherry all round. Then they tackled details of organization which would have to be altered, and the convenience of Linnaeus's plan came out. It was only a case of altering the word "House" to "Lodge" on the handbills. Miss Come could personally do two hundred of them, and Mrs. Naylor's younger children could distribute them on their afternoon walks. There would be notices in the shops and the papers, and after all that, if anybody went to the wrong house, the one gate was only two hundred yards from the other. It remained to be decided where they would put the marquee, the teas and the band, matters which the Bexes were requested to consider at their own convenience. So the crisis was averted, and the practical business of the Committee was finished before the sherry.

Mrs. McGoldrick thought the sherry ought to be finished too. As they sipped sociably at their third round, Wendy Nichol-Jervis said to Lucy, "You'll be interested to hear we've had police all over the place."

"Oh, have you? Then did your father go again about the—"

"The monkshood? No. But you were quite right, and he would have gone, only they were on to it already. A Guard turned up just after you had gone."

"How clever of them!" said Lucy, impressed. "Somehow, one doesn't expect them to detect like that in real life."

"Well, they didn't really. They were put on the track by Larry Quin."

"I never thought of him."

"He knew about it through his father."

"Yes, of course."

"You know," said Wendy, "I'm afraid Larry thinks people might be blaming him for what happened. I expect that was why he was anxious to set the police on a new tack."

This had begun as a private conversation, but naturally by this time everybody was listening. The facts of the tragedy were now public. Tuesday's evening papers had made something of a splash with MONKSHOOD CAUSES DEATH OF TITLED WOMAN, and the *Irish Times* (which stands for culture) printed on Wednesday a short paragraph headed ARTIST'S EVIDENCE IN MONKSHOOD MYSTERY, and containing a nice compliment to Miss FitzEustace. The papers labeled the affair a mystery, and were too discreet to print any conjectures about where the monkshood had come from. But Lucy found that everybody in Clonmeen knew how Dunne's was involved.

"What a mercy if they can prove it didn't come from there!" exclaimed Mrs. Naylor. "But, Miss Nichol-Jervis, dear, what makes you think your father's plant had anything to do with it?"

Wendy told her all about "bikh" and the peculiarly poisonous properties of *Aconitum ferox*, and about its having disappeared with the fig crop on the night before the tragedy.

"Coincidence," said Mr. Naylor.

"And sure, even if it was taken from your place," said Mrs. Naylor, "how could it have got to the Hall?"

Colonel Murray cleared his throat. "There are lots of possibilities. Suppose something like this happened: some blackguard—I beg your pardon, ladies—some ill-disposed person uprooted the monkshood thinking it would look pretty in his front parlor in a vase. He cut the roots off and dropped them in the road. Then along comes some other irresponsible opportunist—Hrrrhm!—picks the roots up, sells them to Dunne as horseradish for a penny, Dunne sells them to the Osmunds for fivepence, and there you are."

"But that doesn't let the Dunnes out," said Mrs. Naylor.

"They wouldn't be buying horseradish," said Wendy. "They grow their own."

"They might have happened to run out of it."

"If you once plant horseradish," said Mr. Lynch, with feeling, "you'll never run out of it."

Miss Cuffe said she would tell them what she thought: "I think Colonel Murray's probably right about the roots of *Aconitum ferox* having been dropped in the road. But then, suppose Dunne's boy comes along on his bicycle. He falls off. All his groceries are upset out of his basket, and when he picks them up he picks up the *Aconitum* along with them. Or, more likely still, he rides past, he happens to look back, he sees the roots lying in the road and thinks he must have dropped them out of his, basket, goes back and picks them up, and includes them with the rest of the horseradish he was delivering at the Hall."

"But what time do you think the plant was taken?" said Mrs. McGoldrick to Wendy.

"The police were asking that, but we've no idea. It might have been any time between when we all went in that evening and early next morning."

"But it was still there in the afternoon? In fact, you showed it to us."

"So we did."

"Well, Dunne delivers to us in the morning. Don't they to you, Miss Bex?" Lucy nodded. "And I suppose the boy went to the Hall then too."

"Unless they rang up the shop later on."

"Oh, you daren't do that nowadays," said Mrs. McGoldrick and Lucy together. "Saturday morning is their time to deliver to this district, ever since they gave up the van."

"In that case," pronounced Colonel Murray, "either it wasn't your *Aconitum ferox* Miss Nichol-Jervis, or it didn't come from Dunne's."

"But shall we ever know?" asked Wendy unhappily. Lucy, who had not felt inclined to join in the argument, was sharply reminded that for Wendy the problem was going to be personal.

Linnaeus had been fumbling for his pocket book, and now produced an envelope with the back closely scribbled over.

"Here's something I copied out today at lunch time," he said. "I dropped in at the National Library to look up *Aconitum,* and I found some interesting information about *Aconitum ferox.* The police will be able to find out if it really was that variety, that is, if they know their job." He read aloud: " 'Besides aconitine, this plant contains another alkaloid, more violent and rapid in its effects; it is given the name of nepaline or pseudoaconitine. Nepaline is more soluble than aconitine in water, alcohol, benzine and chloroform. In contact with azotic acid, and the alcoholic solution of potassium, there is produced a violet coloration, whereas in the same circumstances aconitine gives no colored reaction.' That means, you see, that there's a simple chemical test they can apply to the—er 'fragments that remain.' "*

Everybody looked impressed. Even Mr. Lynch murmured, "Is that so?" with no ironic inflection. Mrs. Naylor declared that science was wonderful. Miss Cuffe thought Linnaeus ought to mention it to the police, just in case they did not know, and, as he seemed to be

*A translation from: *Des Plantes Vénéneuses et des empoisonnements qu'elles déterminent* by Charles Cornevin, 1893.

lacking in public spirit, she privately decided to go round to the barracks tomorrow about a permit to cut down her old thorn tree, and just drop a hint.

But now a gradual tingeing of the atmosphere with a smell of frying made felt the approach of Mrs. McGoldrick's dinner hour and reminded the others of their own. The Committee drank up its heel taps and adjourned, all taking leave with handshaking in a very good humor. There was first the business of seeing the Naylors off in their donkey cart, which was a wartime joke. Then Miss Cuffe mounted her bicycle and rode off, waving. Then Wendy discovered the two hundred handbills that Miss Cuffe had left behind and cycled madly after her. Colonel Murray asked Mr. Lynch if he was going his way, and Mr. Lynch was, so they strolled off together, a rather odd couple, and a walking tribute to the conciliating virtues of gardening.

The Bexes were the last to go. Lucy had lingered behind on purpose. There was something on her mind to ask Mrs. McGoldrick, and she seized this opportunity.

"By the way, Mrs. McGoldrick, do you remember—I don't suppose you do, because it's ages ago—but, casting your mind back to your Book Sale, do you happen to remember who bought the book Linnaeus gave? A book called *Poisonous Plants*. It's awful of him, but after all this he rather wants it back."

"No, I don't," said Linnaeus. "What put that into your head?" Lucy trod on his toe.

"But I can tell you that, as it happens," said Mrs. McGoldrick, "and it's rather a sad coincidence. It was poor Lady Madeleine."

"Really! Are you sure?"

"Certain. You see, it was the last book left—I'm afraid it looked rather learned, Mr. Bex!—and she was the last person to come. Wasn't it very strange now? Almost prophetic."

"Extraordinary," murmured the Bexes. "As you say, a sad coincidence."

But on the way home Lucy said to her brother, "Lin, I have a horrible feeling that there might be something behind this. Anybody who had read *Poisonous Plants* would know about *Aconitum ferox*."

"So what?" said Linnaeus.

"Well, why take that particular plant? It isn't strikingly different from the monkshood you can get growing in lots of gardens. There's nothing about it to attract an ordinary thief."

"Quite," said Linnaeus. "What you're getting at is, it might have been murder?"

"Worse than that," said Lucy. "Lin, do you thank I have invited a murderer to dinner?"

"And if you have, do you think he'll poison us before Lizzie poisons him?"

"It's no laughing matter. I do wish I'd never asked them."

Linnaeus stood still in the road to lecture her. "Now, Lucy, don't you get all worked up over this, and for heaven's sake, woman, don't start suspecting everyone. If it wasn't an accident—which still seems likely—it could have been done by any of half a dozen people from Miss FitzEustace to Larry Quin. Anybody could have read *Poisonous Plants,* the maids, or visitors to the house, or somebody who dipped into it at the Sale. And anyway, we knew the Osmunds knew about *Aconitum ferox,* because they were with us on Saturday. If you want to suspect some-body, why not put your money on the cook? Look at her, going off like that! As for giving those two poor chaps a chance of a decent dinner, you did the only Christian thing."

"Do you really think so?"

"I do. Listen, Lucy, on another matter altogether, I hope it won't be a frightful bore for you, our having the Flower Show."

Lucy's mind was successfully diverted. The rest of the short way passed in an argument about where they would put the band. Linnaeus wanted to station it at the far corner of the paddock, where it would be as barely as possible not on Mr. McGoldrick's land.

When they reached home there was an even more successful diver-sion. Old Lizzie was standing at the front door, looking out for them. As soon as she saw them she shrieked,

"Tellygram! From Master Ivor!"

"Lizzie! Hurry up! Tell us what it says!" Telegrams always came over the telephone and so were public property.

"Two weeks' leave. Arrive Thursday."

"Tomorrow! How splendid! Lizzie, I can smell something burning!" Lizzie made a mad dash back to her stove, while Lucy and Linnaeus went indoors rejoicing.

CHAPTER X
The Next of Kin

MRS. MCGOLDRICK'S sherry and Ivor's telegram combined to hearten the Bexes for hospitality. It looked as if they would have uphill work. Lucy knew she could count on Lord Barna's social tact, but Mr. Osmund had struck her as rather dour, and she could hardly expect much from him in his bereavement. However, it was only too obvious that both men were glad to escape for a short time from Annalee Hall, and that it was a relief to them to talk on any indifferent subject to people unconnected with the tragedy.

They were a queer pair to be so thrown on each other for consolation. Otway Osmund was a solemn person, with dignity rather than charm. Lord Barna, even in mourning, could not quite suppress his native grace and gaiety. Osmund made him look frivolous by comparison. It was natural for Osmund to be the more deeply affected by their common loss, but it also seemed to Lucy that he was more at home with sorrow, perhaps from always having taken life heavily. Without Lady Madeleine they certainly had little in common, and as the evening wore on, it was evident that they got on each other's nerves.

But at their first arrival all was peace. While Lord Barna was telling Linnaeus how splendid this was of Lucy, Osmund said to her, holding her hand,

"Real kindness like yours, Miss Bex, is a rare experience." Lucy protested. "Yes, indeed," he declared. "I am sorry, but you are old fashioned. Doing good to one's neighbor has quite gone out."

"I hope not," said Lucy.

"You may have been fortunate. But when you have lived as long as I have—" He released her hand and shrugged his shoulders. Lucy did not think there could be much difference in their ages, but it was civil of him to pretend.

"You must not talk like that," she said briskly. "Linnaeus and I are very glad if we can be of some practical use. But we know that nobody—we know how little one can do—" she tailed off into embarrassed attempts at condolences. Osmund murmured, "Thank you, thank you," and there they hung for an awkward moment, till Lord Barna relieved the strain by asking how the Flower Show meeting had gone.

The Flower Show lasted them through the soup course. The Bexes were full of the latest changes; Otway Osmund had a taste for the details of organization, and Lord Barna was interested in any activity that involved Wendy Nichol-Jervis.

Lucy had told Linnaeus of the romance, with a warning that officially he was not to know anything about it. This came easy to a person of his detachment. His own married life had been brief, and he had buried all interest in such matters when Ivor's mother died.

However, as soon as Wendy's name was mentioned, Mr. Osmund remarked,

"Now, that's somebody whose acquaintance I shall have to cultivate."

Lord Barna laughed self-consciously. Lucy said, "The Nichol-Jervises are very old friends of ours."

"That," said Osmund, "is a recommendation. You may be surprised at my interest in them, but I am going to surprise you still more. Roland here has found time, in the last few days, to get engaged to Miss Wendy."

The Bexes looked as surprised as they could and murmured congratulations.

"Thank you," Osmund sighed. "My own reactions are of small importance. One ought, perhaps, to be glad of a reminder that life, after all, goes on." He sounded reproachful, but softened it by adding, "They have my blessing, for what it is worth."

"Great girl, Wendy!" said Linnaeus heartily. "Lovely looking and full of go. Runs that big house and practically runs the village. Do anything for anybody. Oh, Wendy's a power!"

"She's artistic, too," added Lucy, thinking this would interest Lord Barna. "Did you know she has quite a talent for drawing?"

Linnaeus laughed. "Show them 'Mad-a-gas-car'."

This was a caricature that Wendy had made of Mr. McGoldrick in his charcoal gas-driven van. The guests had already heard all about Mr. McGoldrick in connection with the Flower Show. The Bexes explained that Wendy had drawn this picture of him for Ivor to wear at a competition party, as a badge representing "a name in the news." It was in a little bureau in a corner of the dining-room, so Lucy had only to turn in her chair to get it out for them. After the custom of caricatures, it portrayed

Mr. McGoldrick in a frenzied attitude, with a furious expression. He was shown cursing his van, which had broken down.

It sent Lord Barna into peals of laughter, which scandalized old Lizzie, who was now changing plates. Even Mr. Osmund's melancholy relaxed.

"Expressive line," he commented. "I think I shall recognize McGoldrick, if ever I meet him. I never have, you know."

"Did it get a prize?" asked Lord Barna.

"It ought to have," said Linnaeus. "Lucy wouldn't let Ivor wear it."

"And a good thing too," said Lucy, "because Mr. McGoldrick turned up at the party when everybody thought he was in Drogheda. You see, you can never depend on him."

"He's putting you to a lot of inconvenience over the Flower Show," said Osmund. "It's very public-spirited of you to set such an example of tolerance."

"Oh, all sides rub along all right in Clonmeen," Linnaeus told him. "McGoldrick is, quite the exception. He's a Northerner, of course."

"Politics are the curse of this country," said Osmund, making the recognized gambit for a discussion on the lines customary in Ireland. Everybody begins by voicing what he assumes are the other parties' opinions, without giving away his own. Thus, the Bexes, seeing that Lord Barna was not in the British forces, praised neutrality, while Osmund, glancing round at various photographs of Ivor and other people in uniform, said that, in his view, "Devallera" had missed a great chance. Then Lucy said that nobody could doubt that "Mr. De Valera" represented the feeling of the country generally, Osmund wondered what would happen when all those who had joined the British forces came back to their own country, and Linnaeus spoke soberly of the disillusionments that follow victory.

So far, it was all a harmony based on familiar refrains, with nobody being provocative and no urge to reach any conclusion. Only Lord Barna did not contribute any remark, but he appeared to be enjoying his fruit salad. Lucy, unsuspicious of tension, looked round her table complacently, thinking how well the evening had gone. Osmund went on talking about the war, professing to envy young men their opportunities. He said he did not know how anybody who read the papers could stay at home. "Tunisia! Sicily! What an experience! The Army has no use for an old crock like me, but it's hard to feel you're missing all the fun."

Lord Barna glanced up at him through his eyelashes and said, "Especially when you missed it all last time, too."

"Last time," said Osmund, "I was in South America." Then he glared at the younger man. "What do you mean?"

If Lord Barna had meant to annoy, he recollected himself.

"Nothing," he said quickly. "You needn't be so touchy, Otway, I didn't mean a thing. No more fruit salad, thank you, Miss Bex, it was delicious."

But Osmund continued irritable. Half to himself, he grumbled, "It doesn't come well from you, of all people."

"All right," said Lord Barna, "I take it back."

"You'd better. Otherwise somebody might start wondering what you think you're playing at, when there's a world war on."

"Why, that's utterly unfair of you, Otway," cried Lord Barna. "Considering it was you who got me articled, and you and Madeleine both advised me not to prejudice my career."

"Need you bring Madeleine into it?" said Osmund, his voice breaking on the name.

The Bexes looked at each other in despair, and though neither Osmund nor Linnaeus had finished their helpings, Lucy was about to suggest going into the other room for coffee, when there was a timely interruption. Old Lizzie put her head in and said,

"If you please, ma'am, there's a man at the door."

"Tell him we never give help—" Lucy began, but Lizzie shook her head.

"It isn't a beggar, ma'am. It's somebody for Mr. Osmund. He says he was sent round here from the Hall."

Osmund blinked at them. "For me? I wasn't expecting—However, I suppose I'd better see what he wants, if Miss Bex will forgive me."

"We were just going into the garden room for coffee," said Lucy. "Will you join us there when you've disposed of your visitor?" Osmund said he would, and went out into the hall, while the others retired through the folding doors to the small back room, where the French windows stood wide open to the garden.

Lord Barna immediately turned to Lucy and flooded her with embarrassing explanations. "Otway doesn't mean all he says, Miss Bex. I ought to have let him alone, I know I ought. Do you ever feel like that, that you just can't resist getting a rise out of a person? Otway always rises. But what he said to me— Matter of fact, at one time I did want to join up, but Madeleine was against it, and then she got

Otway to get me into his firm and pay my fees, and after that I couldn't very well walk out on him, could I?"

Lucy, by now feeling very tired, replied that it was entirely his own affair, which did not seem to satisfy him. But, before he could elaborate, old Lizzie put her head in through the folding doors and signaled to Lucy.

"Mr. Osmund's raging with that fella," she whispered, "and now he's roaring for the other gentleman. Will I tell his lordship to go out to them?"

Osmund had left open the door between the dining room and the hall, so that his voice came clearly through.

"This is outrageous," he was shouting. "An imposition! Blackmail! Where's my nephew?" and, raising his voice, "Roland, here!"

"Oh, God, what is it now?" said Lord Barna, and went to find out. The doors shut behind him, and the Bexes were left in peace in the garden room. Lucy glanced at Linnaeus with raised eyebrows, but only said, "I hope their coffee won't be cold."

"Let's have ours," said Linnaeus. "You can send the rest back to be hotted up."

Lucy poured out coffee and they each took their favorite chairs. With the closing of the dining-room doors the voices in the hall had sunk to a murmur. Remus, the cat, who had made himself scarce for visitors, strolled in through the French windows and jumped on Linnaeus's knee. Dusk deepened in the garden room—in the Emergency, nobody lit a lamp until they had to—and, leaning back restfully, Lucy focused half-closed eyes on the evening star. Honeysuckle on a trellis outside sent in drifts of fragrance. Host and hostess were both nearly asleep when the guests came back.

"My profound apologies, Miss Bex!" Osmund's voice in the shadows made Lucy sit up with a start. "That was not the sort of thing one cares to inflict on one's friends. The responsibility lies with Roland. Hell! Have I broken something? Miss Bex, I beg your pardon. Isn't it rather dark in here?"

"Oh dear," said Lucy. "No, you haven't broken anything, you've only spilled the coffee. I do hope none of it has gone on you. Linnaeus, we must have a light."

"Where have you hid the matches?" asked Linnaeus, a nonsmoker. Lucy said they were in the pewter tankard, or, if not, inside the top of her work basket. They both groped vaguely.

"You got matches, Roland?" said Osmund.

"Left them in my other pocket," said Lord Barna. "What about your own?"

"Empty box."

"Can't find any in the work box," said Linnaeus.

"I said 'basket.' One ought," declared Lucy, "to develop one's sense of touch. Oh, Mr. Osmund, was that your foot?"

"Mind where you walk! There's coffee spilt here."

"Damn! I've pricked myself."

"What's the matter?" inquired a new voice from the windows. "Are you looking for matches? I've a lighter here."

The room was lit for half a second by a blue flicker, which showed the coffee pot overturned on the Indian rug and a splash on Osmund's suit, and a young man just inside the window, shielding the flame from the draft and surveying them with an amused expression.

The light went out again as Lucy clutched at the newcomer.

"Ivor!"

"Wait a sec, Auntie!" he said, and, having located the room's one candle in the first brief light-up, he flicked his lighter at it and they were able to see again, at least to a slight extent.

Lucy embraced him, and turned proudly to the others.

"This is my nephew, whom you've heard so much about. Ivor, how on earth did you get here? The telegram said tomorrow."

"I got a lift in a plane to the North and caught the train from Belfast. Sorry if it's inconvenient."

"Of course it isn't, you silly boy. Only, your sheets won't be aired."

"I expect I'll survive," said Ivor, who had once spent ten hours adrift in the North Sea. But Lucy, looking very worried, went to the door and called out to Lizzie with instructions to hang Master Ivor's sheets on the clotheshorse in the warm kitchen, and heat up enough water for two hot jars.

Osmund and Lord Barna said they must be going. Linnaeus half-heartedly invited them to wait while some more coffee was made, but they were not tempted. Lucy, feeling conscience-stricken, offered to sponge Mr. Osmund's suit, but he said it would be better to let the maid do it at home, where they had electric light. So the Bexes let them go. Lord Barna lingered a moment to say, rather anxiously, to Lucy,

"Now your nephew has come, you mustn't bother about coming over to the Hall in the morning. You'll be much too busy." But Lucy, who had temporarily forgotten all about it, renewed her promise of help, and sent him off with his mind at rest, at least, in that respect.

Linnaeus saw them out by the back way through the garden and locked up the garden doors. Lucy hurried in and out of the kitchen and up and down from Ivor's bedroom with her arms full of bedclothes and towels. As for the returned hero, he fetched a basin of water and a cloth from the scullery and carefully mopped up the coffee.

CHAPTER XI
The Domestic Background

IT IS A PRESUMPTUOUS thing to walk into anybody else's kitchen and order meals. Lucy nerved herself with an effort to face the Osmunds' Norah, who, she knew, would regard her as a busybody. After all, somebody had to interfere.

The returned hero was having breakfast in bed, and Lucy knew better than to send it up before ten, so she left him to the care of old Lizzie, and, having given Mr. Osmund and Lord Barna time to start for their office, she walked over to Annalee Hall.

The shortcut was by the back door of the Bexes' garden, across the paddock, through the fence, round the outside of the Osmunds' walled garden, and across the yard to their kitchen premises. Lucy liked the path—she had been along it often when the Hall belonged to its former owners—and was pleased to find it had not come within the orbit of Lady Madeleine's alterations. There was still valerian growing on the wall, a mat of periwinkle along the bottom of the fence, and the same huge watering-can standing near a funny old iron pump, which was not for water, but for liquid manure from the now empty cow house. The shortcut took you past all the manure heaps, but they were not noisome to a gardener. Lucy was interested to inspect Larry Quin's pit full of compost, neatly covered with a quilt of decaying cabbage leaves. A heap of fresh stable dung beyond it excited her envy; she estimated there was about five pounds' worth at current prices. Through a gate guarded by a sapling rowan tree, she came on to the tradesmen's avenue where it curved round toward the yard. There was a continuation of the path through the shrubbery to the front of the house, but here the evergreens had grown very dense, and the freshly tarred stumps of laurels and laurustinus showed where Larry Quin had recently been hacking a way through. He had not spared an old bay tree that grew convenient to the kitchen window. Lucy reflected that its owners probably did not know how to value it, and broke off a leaf to put in her next stew.

Turning into the yard, she found Larry talking to Norah at the scullery door. It sounded like a quarrel. They broke off short when they heard Lucy's step on the stones. Larry touched his cap civilly and went off, and Norah, looking as if she had not had the last word, glowered after him, as she stood aside for Lucy to come in.

Lucy walked through the scullery into the kitchen, and Norah dusted a chair and placed it for her in the very middle of the floor. Lucy trusted that the housemaid's unbending primness betokened nothing but an earnest desire to make a good impression. Anybody who was not used to the expressions of domestic servants might have taken it for hostility. Thrusting down her rising inferiority complex, Lucy said,

"Thank you, Norah, I don't think I need sit down. I just wondered if I could do any shopping for you, or give you any help about the meals."

"Yes, madam," said Norah unhelpfully.

Lucy glanced round the kitchen for inspiration. It was not very tidy, but one could not be too critical under the circumstances. If there had been the same litter on the table on Saturday, it was easy to see how the horseradish had been accidentally thrown away. Among dirty plates, cloths (impossible to say whether dish, oven, or floor cloths), newspapers, and cabbages brought in by Larry, was spread out a pair of gray flannel trousers. Lucy thought they must be Mr. Osmund's, and asked eagerly if Norah had been able to get the coffee stain out.

"Them's not the master's, them's his lordship's," said Norah, with the air of one who is overworked. "I haven't got around to Mr. Osmund's yet." Lucy reflected that there was not much hope of getting rid of the coffee stain now, if it had not been sponged while it was fresh. However, Mr. Osmund could buy himself a new pair of trousers, and her business was with the inner, not the outer man.

"Well," she said, "what about dinner? Have you settled anything?"

"I'll have to order a joint," said Norah vaguely.

"Yes, certainly. If you haven't got anything yet, it's time to ring up, or they'll have sold out the best cuts. Suppose you get a forequarter of lamb. Then you can roast the leg tonight and stew the chops tomorrow." She was going to add that Norah could take off the flap and stuff it for another day, but decided that this would be beyond the housemaid's powers. "Perhaps," she said, "before we order anything, I'd better see what you've got."

Norah showed her into the larder. As Lord Barna had indicated, it was almost bare. There were, however, possibilities for the seeing eye, in the way of doing up remains of vegetables and sauce. It was when Lucy suggested cauliflower au gratin that she learned the curious fact that the grater had been missing since Monday. That is, Theresa, the cook, had been looking for it in vain when she wanted to grate up some breadcrumbs on Monday morning. The last time it was seen was on Saturday, in connection with the fatal dish of horseradish.

"I was wondering," said Norah, "if I ought to mention it."

"How do you mean?" Lucy asked.

"To the Guards."

"Oh! Oh well, I don't know. It doesn't seem very important."

"I'm sure I've no wish to mix myself up in anything," said Norah, "but the Guards are here every day asking this, that and the other thing, and perhaps they'd have a right to be told."

Lucy considered the question. It did seem possible that the loss of the grater might be significant. Had it been borrowed in order to grate up the monkshood? She did not want to make a lot out of a trifle, so she said with a smile,

"Well, I think perhaps if I were you I would just mention it. The detectives might be able to find it for you."

"Them fellas find anything!" said Norah. "Amn't I after looking everywhere myself?"

"Well, just as you think, Norah, whatever seems best to yourself," said Lucy, meaning these vague expressions to have a conciliatory effect. Returning to the subject of meals, she produced a pencil and paper and jotted down menus for three days ahead. She also made a list of orders for telephoning to the shops.

"Anything else?" she asked, scribbling briskly. "Polishes? Cleaning materials? I suppose you have all those."

Norah asked if she knew of a plumber.

"There isn't a good one locally," said Lucy, stating what was a felt want in Clonmeen. "There's Barney Birdy, but I wouldn't let him into the house if I was you. Is it something urgent?"

"It's the wastepipe of the mistress's handbasin. I mean, the handbasin in her ladyship's room."

"That hardly seems worth getting a man out from town for."

"No, madam. Only, it was the last thing her ladyship said to me, a Sunda'. Whatever took it, the pipe was blocked that afternoon, and had us all running up and down with slop pails. The mistress thought it was my blame, but it was all right that morning, and I doing out the room." Norah oozed self-righteousness. "But that was her ladyship's last words to me, that I should get that basin attended to."

Lucy said she would see about it, but, at the risk of ignoring a death-bed command, she felt that the first thing was to get on to the butcher and grocer before any more of the morning wore away. She asked where she could telephone, and Norah showed her into a back room which contained a small bookshelf and a large desk and was called "the study."

Waiting for the Clonmeen exchange to wake up and put her through, Lucy had time to reflect how soon a house showed signs of having no one to look after it. There was a sickly smell in the hall from a jar of *Lilium regale*. Lady Madeleine must have arranged them. The flower stalks, poked out in a Voguish fan, still held their lines, and nobody had noticed that the flowers were dead. The study had been dusted conscientiously, and the ornaments and photographs, meant to be casually scattered about, were now ranged on bookshelf and mantelpiece with rigid symmetry and too near the edge. A window curtain had come off one of its hooks and hung in clumsy folds. Some reference books on the writing desk were upside down.

The books on the desk were a dictionary, Thom's Directory, and Debrett. Lucy always wanted to see what people read, and, when she had finished telephoning, she could not resist going over to the bookshelf. It was full of recent publications, Book Society choices and bestsellers that Lucy had heard of and not read. She admired the effect of all the bright new bindings, which she could not help contrasting with the shabby collection in the garden room at Annalee Lodge. There was no sign of Linnaeus's copy of *Poisonous Plants*.

Norah had been listening for Miss Bex to finish with the telephone. She opened the study door just as Lucy was on her knees inspecting the bottom shelf.

"Were you looking for something, madam?" she asked.

Lucy jumped and felt fairly caught snooping. Under Norah's mistrustful stare, she said the first thing that came into her head, which was to ask the housemaid if she knew what had happened to Linnaeus's book. Too late she regretted having betrayed such an obvious interest in it, when the title was bound to connect it with the tragedy. Lucy never could acquire the art of pumping people, she always had to ask her questions right out. But it seemed that she was not the only person on that trail.

"*Poisonous Plants*, madam?" repeated Norah. "That might be the book the Guard took away with him yesterday. He has it still. I thought it belonged to the house."

"Oh, it does," Lucy assured her. "My brother gave it to a sale and Lady Madeleine bought it. Then yesterday he wanted to look something up in it. You see, it told all about the monkshood, and I'm afraid, after this dreadful affair, we couldn't help being interested. I expect that's why the police borrowed it too."

"I daresay, madam. But the Guard took it up very careful, and asked me if I'd been dusting it. An' I told him I dusted the shelves every morning regular, and he didn't say much, but I could see he was vexed. And he held the book in his handkerchief and put it in his little bag he had, most particular. By what I understood," said Norah, almost unbending in the drama of her narration, "that fella' was looking for fingerprints."

CHAPTER XII
An Outside Opinion

HAVING SETTLED the affairs of Annalee Hall, Lucy had no more pressing chores to attend to and was free for the long talk with her nephew that she had been looking forward to all morning. She went up and removed a large tray of breakfast things from the foot of his bed, sat down herself, and had a good look at him.

"And how are you, my dear boy?" she demanded. "Oh dear, you always look older than I expect you to." Lucy could never get used to the idea of Ivor as a man; her mental picture of him was still that of a sprawling schoolboy. Nowadays he looked controlled, responsible, grown up. He had improved, but it caused her a pang.

"I'll shave presently," said Ivor, "and that'll take years off me. You look blooming, Aunt Lucy. And now I can see you're going to tell me all the news."

"Of course I am," said Lucy. "Only I don't know where to begin. Oh, first of all, will you be here till Saturday week? We're having the Flower Show."

"I've got a fortnight. Looks as if I can't escape."

"You may well say 'escape.' When I say we're having the Flower Show, I mean we literally are having it. Here. Don't blame me. Your father brought it on us himself." She told him all about Linnaeus's reaction to the factious behavior of Mr. McGoldrick.

"Time someone showed old McGoldrick where he got off," commented Ivor. "Never mind, Aunt Lucy, I'll see you through. Tell me, how's everybody round? How are the Nichol-Jervises?"

"That's another piece of news. Wendy's engaged."

"Is—that—so?" said Ivor. "Since when?"

"It's only just happened. It's to Lord Barna. You know. That was him here last night."

"What! That twirp?"

"You needn't call him names. He's a very nice boy and I'm sure they'll be very happy."

"Oh yeah?" said Ivor. "We hope!" He saw Lucy about to rebuke him for vulgarity and intercepted quickly,

"What were you all up to last night? Was it a party?"

"Not exactly," replied Lucy, looking solemn. "You see, Lady Madeleine Osmund—you know, Mr. Osmund's wife—I wrote all about her. Well, she died in a very tragic way only last Sunday."

"What happened to her?"

"It's rather a mystery. I'll tell you all about it presently. But, on top of that, the cook left. So however it all turns out, I had to see that those two poor men had a decent meal."

"And I'm sure they did," said Ivor. "And who was the gent out in the hall?"

"Oh," said Lucy, remembering, "did you see him? I didn't. I haven't a notion who he was. He came round asking for Mr. Osmund."

"They seemed to be having a bit of a difference," said Ivor. "When I came to the hall door they were swearing at each other so I couldn't make anybody hear."

"So that was why you came in by the garden. Yes, it was rather queer about that man. Come to think of it, they never explained him, but I daresay they would have if you hadn't turned up." Lucy's voice conveyed some unexpressed doubts. After a slight hesitation, she went on, "And there are one or two other things that are queerer than him. In fact, I'd like to know how it all strikes you, bringing a fresh mind to bear."

"Pass me a cigarette," said Ivor, "and tell me all."

Lucy fished Ivor's cigarettes and his useful lighter out of his coat pocket and helped herself. Ivor lit up for both of them. She balanced an ashtray between them, settled herself against the foot of the bed, and began.

"On the face of it," said Lucy, "it's nothing to do with me. I know you and your father think I'm always getting involved in things, but this time it's only been what I really couldn't help. I couldn't have got out of going to the inquest with Miss FitzEustace, and then, what with the Osmunds being next-door neighbors, and Lord Barna getting engaged to Wendy—"

"Who's Miss FitzEustace?" interrupted Ivor.

"Only Miss Milfoyle's latest p.g. She's an artist of sorts. She was painting Lady Madeleine in the Hall garden, and she happened to be there when Lady Madeleine was taken ill. That's the only way she comes into it. At least," said Lucy, remembering the monkshood in church, "she might be a suspect, but she doesn't seem a likely one."

"A suspect?" said Ivor. "Then you're telling me Lady Madeleine was murdered?"

"That's the whole thing," said Lucy unhappily. "We don't know for certain, but it really is beginning to look rather like it."

She saw she had captured Ivor's attention. It was always a satisfaction to Lucy to notice how her brother and her nephew, neither of them good-looking, almost became so when they concentrated on a problem. Ivor smoked and listened with an alert expression, while his aunt, having got into her stride, told the story of the last few days in simple chronological order. In doing so, she found herself seeing things more in perspective, and one feature of the situation, that she had rather forgotten, resumed its original importance.

"If they never find out how those roots got there," she said, "everybody is going to think they came from Dunne's. And that's very hard luck on James and Mrs. Dunne, because I'm perfectly certain they had nothing to do with it."

"But if they can prove by analysis that the roots were the kind of monkshood that only grew at Beechfield, the shop won't come into it at all."

"Yes, they might. Wherever the monkshood roots came from, the horseradish was from Dunne's. The mix-up might have happened either there or at the Hall. But it makes it less likely to have been at Dunne's. From the effects, I feel sure it was *Aconitum ferox*. You see, it wasn't only my idea. The expert evidence struck Larry Quin that way too."

"Smart of him, wasn't it? Look here, do you think he'd know any more than he lets on? Don't the police always suspect people who bob up and offer them information?"

"So they say. It doesn't seem a good reason to me. But I have wondered about Larry. He had a kind of grievance against Lady Madeleine. He wanted to go to England to earn enough money to marry on, and she was doing all she could to stop him getting a permit."

"Could she? Stop him, I mean."

"Well, yes, I think so. They don't like to let a man go if they know there's a job for him here."

"That does seem to give Larry Quin a motive. What's the formula, you know, what a murderer has to have? 'Motive, means and opportunity.' As for means, I suppose he could have helped himself to anything from Beechfield."

"So long as his father didn't catch him. Goodness, Ivor! Suppose it was one of the young Quins who stole the figs. If they took their father's key they wouldn't have to climb in over the tar. My goodness, there would be a row!" The idea of a traitor within Beechfield's own gates seemed to Lucy the worst thing they had thought of yet, for though murder was shocking enough, this was bordering on anarchy.

"I don't understand that fig business," said Ivor. "It doesn't seem to fit in. Can you imagine a man who was planning murder stopping to bother picking fruit? It surely can't have been more than a coincidence."

Lucy mentioned Colonel Murray's theory that the fruit thieves had torn up the flowers and dropped the roots in the road, thus leading to their accidental substitution for the horseradish. On repetition, it did not sound very convincing. The fact that Dunne's delivery boy would have passed much earlier in the day made the accident theory difficult to construct.

"Yes, if I were the police," said Ivor, going back to the beginning, "I'd certainly think it was a point against Larry that he knew all about that plant being particularly poisonous. Of course, what with Question Time and the Brains Trust, you never know what to expect, but I shouldn't think many people round here knew as much botany as that."

"Oh yes, they did. The Nichol-Jervises must have told everybody they took round the garden. You know how one tends to say the same things to everyone who comes. Lots of people had heard about Peter Nichol-Jervis sending seeds home from the Middle East, and last Saturday, at tea, we heard all about bikh all over again: your father and I, and the Osmunds themselves, poor things, and Mrs. McGoldrick and Miss Milfoyle and Miss FitzEustace."

Ivor whistled. "But at any rate, it rules out the maids."

"Don't you be too sure. Larry might easily have talked about it in the kitchen. Didn't I tell you it was the cook that he was courting?"

"Was it indeed?"

"And now she has run away. Doesn't that look bad? Perhaps they did it in collusion."

"Perhaps it was a case of 'the woman tempted me.' Is Theresa a looker?"

"You might think so. I should call her flighty. But I must say that, of the two of them, Norah, the house parlormaid, strikes me as much more sinister."

"Suspect number three," said Ivor. "Bracketing Larry and Theresa together as number two."

"Then who's your number one?"

"Miss FitzEustace. In order of mention, not in order of importance. All you really had against her was being seen in possession of the monkshood."

"She's rather sinister too," said Lucy reflectively. "One of these spinsters, you know, though I say it as shouldn't. She seemed very interested in Lady Madeleine. And there she was at the Hall, all Sunday morning. She could easily have slipped into the kitchen and left the grated up roots instead of the horseradish."

"Yes, but she couldn't have known they were going to have horseradish."

"Oh yes, she could. Anyone who's ever done the housekeeping might have guessed that. Ordering meals," said Lucy, launching on a favorite topic, "is like free will and predestination. You think you can have what you like, and then you find it's all dictated by circumstances. The weekend before a bank holiday you have to think about having something cold for Monday. There isn't enough on lamb and nobody wants to eat cold mutton. Pork's no good in August, and you can't get ham at present. So you see it just has to be beef, and now that nobody has any mustard, horseradish naturally goes with it."

"Sounds simple," said Ivor skeptically. "I should think it would be a bit too simple for a jury, especially as they don't have women on them over here."

"Well, for that matter," said Lucy, "she might have happened to overhear the order at Dunne's. She often does errands in the village for Miss Milfoyle. Or she might have hung about and seen when the butcher's boy delivered beef. When he called at Miss Milfoyle's, the joint for Annalee Hall would be in his bicycle basket, with a docket pinned on it for anybody to read."

"All right, all right. I forgot that everybody in Clonmeen knows all about everybody else. But wait a bit. You said she was only asked to Annalee Hall on the Saturday afternoon."

"She practically asked herself. Now, that was queer too, if you come to think of it. I remember thinking at the time that she seemed determined to get a commission out of Lady Madeleine."

"And did she know then about the monkshood?"

"She did. We were talking about it at tea."

"Well, all I can say is, she must have done some quick thinking, and she had better luck than the average murderer could depend on. She'd have looked pretty silly if anyone had caught her pulling up the plant."

"But what I think is, she picked it up in the road. I don't believe she planned the murder beforehand, but if she had a motive that we don't know about, then having the opportunity presented to her like that might easily have put murder into her head."

"Well, find her a good strong motive, and I'll believe you," said Ivor. "You'll know better than I would how to start delving into Miss FitzEustace's murky past."

"I don't really suspect her at all," said Lucy, with feminine inconsistency. "I should say it was much more likely Norah. Remember, it was Norah who brought the roots in from the rubbish heap."

"You're down on Norah, aren't you? I don't see how she could have got hold of the roots."

"Why not through Larry?"

"But Theresa is Larry's girl."

"Isn't that just why he might have preferred to work through Norah? Who knows what hold he might have had on her? Norah may have been in love with him herself."

"Does she look that sort?"

"Well," said Lucy, "she certainly looks blighted. It might be love or it might be indigestion. You can't always tell. And when I went over there this morning, she and Larry were quarreling."

"You can't denounce her on spec," said Ivor. "As one who is

fighting for the four freedoms, etc., etc., I won't have it. You must find me evidence."

"I'll tell you one thing. It doesn't count for much, but it is another way she might have known about *Aconitum ferox*. It's all in a book called *Poisonous Plants* that your father gave to Mrs. McGoldrick's sale and Lady Madeleine bought. Ever since then it's been lying about at Anna-lee Hall. Well, today I tried to borrow it back again, and Norah found me looking for it on the shelf, and when I asked for it by its title, she looked daggers at me. And what do you think?" said Lucy, working up to her climax. "The police had taken it."

"I daresay they wanted to read the subject up for themselves. No, Aunt Lucy, you haven't got anything on the sinister Norah. But we haven't discussed the most obvious suspects of all."

"Whom do you mean?"

"Lord Barna and Mr. Osmund. Or Mr. Osmund and Lord Barna, if you prefer them in that order. It's all very well putting it on the servants, but it's just as likely to have been a family matter. It's generally people's nearest relatives who want to murder them."

"That's a solemn thought," said Lucy, smiling uneasily.

"Yes, but really, Aunt Lucy. Everything we've said about the others having motive, means, and opportunity applies to them. Lord Barna might have wanted money; Mr. Osmund might be wanting to marry somebody else. They both knew about the monkshood; they had the book in the house and they went to the tea party. Either of them could easily have climbed the Beechfield wall. They knew what there would be for Sunday dinner. They could have sneaked into the kitchen any time and switched the roots."

Lucy said, "I have faced the possibility of it being one of those two. I even mentioned it to your father."

"What does he think?"

"He doesn't think it's more than a possibility."

She looked very serious as she considered this aspect of the problem. Neither of them spoke for a minute or so. Then it was Ivor who summed up cheerfully:

"Well, there you are: five suspects. Or is it six? I've lost count. I must say I don't see how you're going to pin it on any of them. And after all, it may have been an accident. Or a stunt that went wrong. Suppose one of the servants had a grievance and wanted to make her sick, by way of getting their own back."

"Oh, surely they wouldn't do that?" Lucy was shocked. "I feel sure it will turn out to have been an accident, though. The most extraordinary accidents do happen to people. Not long ago I was reading in a booklet from an insurance company about a man who was bitten by his own false teeth."

"Doesn't that just show you?" said Ivor.

Lucy picked up the ashtray off the eiderdown, walked over to the open window and emptied the ashes of their two cigarettes over a climbing geranium. Beyond the garden and the paddock she could see the stone wall of the Hall garden, with unpruned tops of apple trees showing over it, and, beyond again, the slate roofs of the house. It was a severe gray stone house, softened by its setting in foliage, but not a homely place. After this, she wondered, would people say it was haunted? Turning back to the bedroom, she said to Ivor,

"Now that I've told you the whole story, I don't want to talk about it any more. It isn't pleasant to harbor such thoughts about neighbors and people who've been in your own home. It's too serious a matter for guessing. We must just wait till the police come to the end of their inquiries. From what I gathered this morning, they are doing a good deal of unobtrusive investigating over there at the house. So I should think we could leave it to them, and I hope they'll be quick about it. I'm going now. It's time for you to get up."

CHAPTER XIII
A Leading Suspect

AFTER THEIR MORNING'S TALK, which did not seem to have thrown much light on the mystery, Lucy felt she had better give her nephew something else to think about. Over lunch, she enumerated little jobs she wanted done about the house.

"I do wonder if you could do anything with the wireless," she said. "Your father gets so cross at not being able to hear the news. Especially now it's so good. I believe he'd rather have worse news and better reception. And, as you see, this clock has stopped, and I expect you noticed the weighing machine in the bathroom isn't working. Oh, that reminds me, over at the Hall there's a handbasin with the waste pipe stopped up. I promised to look at it and never did. Perhaps you'd come over with me and fix it for them tomorrow."

"Thank you very much," replied her nephew sarcastically. "Looks as if I shan't have much difficulty occupying myself on leave. Anybody else round here require a plumber, do you suppose? As a matter of fact, I was thinking of going round to Beechfield this afternoon, if I could have my half day off."

"That's all right, darling boy," Lucy beamed at him fondly. "They'll be so delighted to see you. They'll want you to stay tea, so I won't expect you back till dinner time."

"O.K. But there's no point in going up there too soon after lunch. I'll have a look at the wireless first." It should be fairly clear by now that Ivor was every aunt's ideal nephew. Lucy reflected with pride how well she had brought him up.

So in the afternoon Ivor went off to Beechfield, starting by way of the village, where he hoped to get something the wireless wanted. Lucy might have gone with him, but the world had been so much with her lately that she preferred the peace of her own garden. Now that she had an afternoon to herself, she might bottle the tomatoes, or tackle the arrears of household mending. She decided on the mending. In the Emergency, when old sheets and towels were irreplaceable, the laundry, with worn-out machinery that could not be replaced either, was making worse inroads on them than ever.

Half an hour after Ivor had gone, there came the first ping-ping of the telephone bell, which always punctuated his leaves. Mrs. McGoldrick, having met him in the village, had promptly nailed him for a tennis party on the following afternoon, and was now ringing up to invite Lucy and Linnaeus too. Lucy was glad to hear that Ivor had capitulated, so that it was not incumbent on her to try and wriggle out of the invitation. So she put off the tomato bottling till Saturday, and accepted with thanks for herself, after explaining, what Mrs. McGoldrick already knew, that Linnaeus's work kept him too late.

She rejoiced all the more in having a quiet afternoon all to herself. But as she sat over her sewing, Lucy could not prevent her mind meandering back over the mystery. Sewing, and even more so knitting, conduces to aimless thinking; the occupation of one's hands seems to propel one's thoughts along already worn grooves. In spite of her resolve not to discuss the affair, she could not help wondering, for instance, about last night's unexplained visitor. She even formed some lurid suppositions based on overhearing Mr. Osmund use the word "blackmail". Then it occurred to her that the man might have been a plain clothes detective. Had he come round with news of a fresh development?

Tea came as a distraction. She gladly piled away the linen and took up *Persuasion,* and sat on afterwards reading further chapters. She had by no means exhausted the charms of solitude when she heard a step, and looked up to see Lord Barna hovering at the edge of the lawn. He must have come from the Hall by the shortcut and let himself in by the garden door.

He greeted her with, "How nice you look! So cool and serene. So restful to the sight of one who has just traveled out in the bus."

Lucy had closed her book with a suppressed sigh, but the young man's compliment inclined her kindly toward him. She asked if he had had tea.

"Yes, thanks. At least, I had a drink. May I sit on this?" He dragged round one end of a heavy garden seat and sat down on it with due regard for his city trousers. "Miss Bex, I had to come back and apologize for last night's shemozzle."

Lucy murmured politely that he need not have bothered.

"Well, but you must have wondered. That fellow at the door, I mean. It was disgraceful."

Trying hard to suppress all appearance of curiosity, Lucy said, "I felt so sorry for poor Mr. Osmund. It's a shame for people to persecute him at such a time."

"Oh, it's me he's persecuting," said Lord Barna airily. "I'm the party responsible, so I thought I'd better come and explain. Otway thought so too. He as good as ordered me over here, when I'd already decided to come. I suppose you guessed what last night's intruder was after?"

"Wasn't he just a beggar?" said Lucy innocently. "We get so many of them."

"Ah, not at all. He was a dun. After me for a bill. Don't look so alarmed, Miss Bex! I haven't come to touch you."

"I did not suppose you had," said Lucy rather coldly.

"He asked for Otway because he thought that was his best hope of getting his money. Well, I suppose it was, too, because in the end old Otway paid him off. But it does make me furious. These chaps have absolutely no sense of decency."

Lucy said nothing. In all her conjectures about Mr. Osmund's caller, this explanation had never entered her head. She had moved all her life in prosperous *bourgeois* circles where everybody's credit was sound, and to her the idea of leaving a bill unpaid until you were approached by a debt collector was simply unthinkable. She sat still, trying to adjust her outlook.

Lord Barna, immediately sensitive to disapproval, searched her face, fixing her with large, serious eyes, and renewed his explanation.

"You mustn't think I've been piling up debts regardless. It isn't as easy as Otway thinks to keep on the right side. What I've got of my own, my dividends and so forth, doesn't bring in more than about two-fifty a year. Doesn't leave much margin, as things are nowadays. Madeleine understood. She was much more extravagant than me, only she had more to start with. She didn't make a crime of it if one happened to be slightly overdrawn. She often helped me out till the end of the quarter, and of course I paid her back, if I could get her to take it. Now Otway has the nerve to call it 'sponging on a woman.' " He dug an indignant heel into the lawn. After a pause, in which Lucy failed to say anything sympathetic, he went on,

"But what I want to tell you about is this last unfortunate business. It was all a misunderstanding. The bill just happened to get overlooked, not by me, by Madeleine. It was like this: last birthday I gave a party in my flat. Madeleine came, but she didn't bring old Otway, I daresay she thought she'd enjoy it more without him. Well, you know what happens. Twice as many people turned up as I'd ever invited, and we had to keep sending out for more drinks, and the bill was mounting up to something colossal. Then Madeleine nobly said she'd stand me the whole thing as a birthday present. So when the bill came in I just posted it on to her, and naturally I thought it'd been settled long ago. She must have forgotten about it. She was awfully casual, poor darling." Lucy thought inconsequently that the last sentence provided Lady Madeleine with an epitaph.

"I wish to God," said Lord Barna, "if this business had to crop up, it had come at any other time. It's given old Otway a splendid text for a sermon on riotous living. I believe he's hurt because we had the party without him. Riotous living! He doesn't know the A.B.C. of it. I could take him places—not in Dublin, though. But anyway, I've done with all that now. Before this damned demand came in I was even reducing my overdraft."

He had stopped scrutinizing Lucy and seemed to be brooding on some inward vision. Relieved of his hypnotic gaze, Lucy was able to notice what a hole his heel had dug in the lawn. Quite unconsciously, he was screwing away at it most methodically. She longed to tell him to stop, but instead she said gently,

"I am sorry to hear you are in money difficulties. You have a responsibility now toward Wendy."

"I know I have." His voice sounded very solemn. "You needn't think I'm asking Wendy to marry me on two-fifty a year. Once I'm out of articles I shall start earning a salary. But as a matter of fact, I shall be a bit better off from now on, because of poor Madeleine. What she had from our family will come to me. So old Otway will get his money back in a month or two, whenever the lawyers have finished."

"Very well," said Lucy, feeling dreadfully priggish. "Then now is your chance to live within your income, before you get in the habit of spending a larger sum. So do try, won't you? I don't want to lecture you, but these things are important."

Lord Barna looked up at her, and said with his sweetest smile, "I like you to lecture me, Miss Bex. If I had been brought up by you, I should be a much more admirable sort of person. Like that nephew of yours who found us all messing about in the dark and got us a light. He impressed me. He did really."

"You must meet him properly," said Lucy. "It's a pity he isn't in this afternoon."

"No it isn't," said Lord Barna. "I was hoping to find you alone. I wanted your advice, and I still do. May I go on?"

Lucy glanced at her pile of sheets and towels, wondering if she dared take them up again, in case he was going to be long. But it sounded too serious for that, so she folded her hands again and leaned back in her deck-chair. The shade of the apple tree under which they were sitting was moving round; it only covered her face and soon she would be in the full sun, but it was the kindly evening sun. The air was very still and the sky seemed as empty as ever. When was it ever going to rain again?

"You see," Lord Barna was saying, "making all due allowance for old Otway being on edge, he doesn't exactly behave as if he wanted me. This last row hasn't mended matters. I often think I'd better go."

Lucy could understand that. She said;

"I should think that, now the first few days are over, Mr. Osmund might certainly prefer to be alone. And after all, you will be in close touch through your office."

"Oh yes, we shall. But there's something else now, that makes me think perhaps I ought after all to keep on here. I don't think Otway has grasped it yet, luckily for him. Miss Bex, did you know there's a theory that someone poisoned Madeleine on purpose?"

Lucy might have pretended incredulity, but her face, as usual, gave her away, and the young man watching her did not wait for her to frame a tactful reply. With a hysterical laugh, he went on,

"It's a bit too much, isn't it? As if we hadn't enough to worry us! The police have got this ridiculous idea into their heads, and they just can't let us alone. Oh, I know all about what they've been after at Beechfield. Now, it seems they've proved to their own satisfaction that it was that plant, of all plants. You know, what's its name? Bikh. So then they say, how did it come to the Hall? Not in Dunne's grocery basket. So they keep nosing round and asking Norah questions and you can see them thinking the worst. It's no good arguing with them. I suppose they think it might have been me or Otway as well as anyone."

Lucy longed to be able to contradict him roundly, but handicapped by lifelong habits of sincerity she made a lame reply.

"It can only be a day or two before everything is cleared up."

Lord Barna hardly seemed to hear her. But after a moment he straightened his shoulders and spoke more steadily.

"The police haven't told me to stay put," he said, "but I know damn well they're keeping an eye on me: It might look bad to go away, even only to Dublin."

"Why not try and see what happens?"

"I don't know. There's a morbid fascination about this place, I suppose. I feel if anything develops I'd like to be around."

"Well, you know best," said Lucy. It was not the first time she had been asked to advise someone who only wanted her to agree with him. The sun had now come round the branches and shone full in her eyes. She sat up and shaded them with her hand.

"I am so sorry for you," she said. "Both."

Lord Barna now became remorseful. "I oughtn't to have bothered you. Thank you for listening. How silly that sounds, it's what they say on the wireless. Miss Bex—"

"Yes?"

"You don't think I'm a murderer? I mean, do I look the type?"

His laugh warned her of returning hysteria, and she said "Nonsense!" sharply. He still sat there, and Lucy, blinking in the sunlight, began to wonder if he would ever go. Then she heard the rattle of the garden windows, and turned to see Ivor coming toward them.

"Here's my nephew at last," she said with relief. "Ivor, you are just in time to meet Lord Barna properly and offer your congratulations on his engagement."

"Roland, please," said Lord Barna pleasantly. The two young men shook hands with some formality.

Looking at them together, Lucy regretfully admitted to herself that nobody could call Ivor handsome. He was personable, quite good-looking enough for Clonmeen, but grace and elegance were not his attributes, nor could one derive any aesthetic satisfaction from the shape of his head and hands. It so happened that he was wearing his very worst clothes, those remnants to which he had been reduced through not being allowed to wear British uniform in a neutral country and not having any Irish clothes coupons. So that, in addition to the physical contrast, Roland was dressed like a gentleman and Ivor like a tramp.

Blessings on Ivor, all the same, for putting an end to the strain of a serious conversation. Even the suspect shed his gloom, or concealed it with his habitual cordiality.

"You and Wendy are old friends, aren't you?" he said to Ivor. "I've often heard her speak of you."

"I've heard her mention you, too," said Ivor. "I've been up at Beechfield all afternoon." He grinned amiably. "Matter of fact, I want to borrow your girl for the evening. Glad I ran into you."

Roland looked surprised.

"It's this way," said Ivor. "Wendy's uncle or godfather or someone has sent her tickets for the Louth Hunt Ball."

"Oh, yes?" said Roland.

"Seems a pity to waste them. The old boy's going to be there with a party, and Wendy doesn't like to disappoint him. She didn't know how to get out of it. You see, he doesn't know about her engagement yet."

"Oh, I see."

"Sure you don't mind? Wendy was trying to get you on the phone, but you were out. I suppose you were over here. However, I'll ring up and tell her it's O.K. by you."

"Oh, certainly," said Roland. "Hope you have a good time. I must go now. Good-bye, Miss Bex." He took himself gracefully away.

Ivor looked at Lucy. "You needn't look so old-fashioned at me, Aunt."

"It has been borne in on me this afternoon," replied Lucy, "that I am

old-fashioned. Do you really think you ought to take Wendy out dancing, under all the circumstances?"

"What circumstances? If you mean Lady Madeleine, Wendy hardly
knew her. If you mean her engagement, well, the noble Earl doesn't
seem to object."

"Doesn't Mrs. Nichol-Jervis?"

"Not she. It was her idea."

"Really? Then there's not much point in my saying anything."

"Of course not, Auntie. It's the best dance this leave, and it'd be a
crime to miss it. Where's my dress suit? I hope to goodness you've kept
the moth out of it."

CHAPTER XIV
Going All Over It Again

HOWEVER MUCH she disapproved of her nephew's behavior, Lucy not
only produced his dress suit immaculate but wrested his dinner out of
Lizzie an hour before the usual time. Then she walked down with him to
the bus stop, where they met Wendy. Ivor had covered his evening dress
with a multi-stained and creased old mackintosh; the heels of his dancing pumps stuck out of either pocket. Wendy was all gleaming satin
under a fur coat; one hand carefully lifted her long skirt out of the dust,
disclosing strong brogue shoes, the other clutched an attache-case full of
items to add to her toilette in the cloakroom. That was how people went
to dances in the Emergency.

The bus they were waiting for arrived from town, bringing Linnaeus
back from business. He had stayed late to catch up with work he had
shelved for the Flower Show meeting the day before. He and Lucy saw
the revelers off.

They did not see them again till eight o'clock next morning, when
they returned home, literally, with the milk. After the dance ended, in
the small hours, they failed to secure a taxi, and there seemed nothing for it but to walk, at least, until the first bus services began. They
walked out of Dublin as far as where the houses space out among not
yet built-over fields. Here Wendy, who was a mine of local knowledge,
remembered that a Clonmeen dairy farmer had rented grazing. They

found him just as he was finishing his early morning milking, and he drove them home in his cart.

But Lucy and Linnaeus, after the dancers had gone, walked soberly home. At dinner, Lucy told her brother about her interview with Lord Barna, and they had the family satisfaction of shaking their heads over him together.

They heard the nine o'clock news at eight o'clock, owing to double summer time in England. The wireless, benefited by Ivor's skill, articulated clearly: the Russian advance continued; the Germans were evacuating Sicily; ninety U-boats had been sunk in three months. Afterwards, as they sat on in the dusk economizing their candle, Lucy asked,

"Why should the idea of one murder upset us, considering what is happening to millions of people all over the world?"

"It's something our imaginations can take in, I suppose," said Linnaeus. "Besides, suffering doesn't increase numerically. What happens to one is as bad for him or her as if it was happening to millions. What happens to millions is no worse for them individually than if it happened to one."

"You surely won't pretend that killing on a large scale leaves you indifferent."

"No, but logically one should not be more disturbed by it than by murder next door."

Appealing to logic was a pet habit with Linnaeus that did not impress his sister. "The two things are quite different," she declared. "To be strictly honest, I don't mind as much about Lady Madeleine as I do about any unknown soldier. I hardly knew her and I didn't care for her. But I do mind this atmosphere of suspicion being created all round us."

"Ah, that's another matter. It certainly is desirable that the mystery should be cleared up."

"Desirable! I should think so! We shall all go mad if it isn't. Look at those two men at the Hall. You could see last night that they were ready to jump down each other's throats. It's sheer nerves, of course. And look at me and Lord Barna this afternoon. I didn't know what to say to him. How could I pretend I had no idea of it's being murder?"

"I gather he thinks it wasn't?"

"He said not, but he was only talking. It was dreadful. He wanted me to agree with him and say, 'No, of course not, it couldn't have been anything but an accident,' but somehow I couldn't get the words out. I was thinking all the time, 'I wonder is this really all you know about it?' "

"Very embarrassing," said Linnaeus dryly. "But why have you suddenly fixed on him?"

"I haven't fixed on him!" Lucy snapped. As she had admitted, the uncertainty was telling on her temper. In spite of her resolve not to gossip about the tragedy, here they were back at the unavoidable topic, and as the argument proceeded without making progress, each of them got impatient with the other.

"If it was murder," said Lucy, "it could have been him as much as anyone else. I don't suspect him particularly, poor boy. But now they know it was *Aconitum ferox*, there doesn't seem much chance that it was a mistake."

"As you say, it's hard to conceive how or when an accidental substitution could have occurred."

Remus, the cat, invited himself on to Linnaeus's knee. Linnaeus cocked his leg at the angle which Remus found most comfortable, and sat stroking meditatively. Lucy, who was under the illusion that she could knit in the dark, rummaged in her wool bag.

"I'll tell you something else," she said presently. "It only occurred to me this afternoon, and it's another thing that looks bad. Do you remember what the expert said about the cook's evidence? I mean, how she said she served half the roots as sauce on Saturday, and he said they wouldn't be poisonous if they were boiled. Well, I was thinking how you make horseradish sauce. You don't boil it. You mix it with vinegar and just heat it up gently, or else you do it with cream and don't heat it at all."

"What you're getting at is, it wasn't the same horseradish?"

"It couldn't have been. Otherwise, why didn't anybody get ill on Saturday night? But do you see what that means? Theresa said she grated all the roots up together on Saturday, so that when the monkshood got mixed up with Sunday's lot, it must have been ready grated. What I feel is, roots might have got mixed up with each other by accident, but if somebody grated up some monkshood separately, it must have been on purpose to mix it with the horseradish."

Linnaeus professed to have thought of that himself.

"It seemed probable from the first that the roots were grated. Horseradish and monkshood roots aren't so very alike. There may have been cases of mistakes, but you'd expect anyone with normal senses to notice the difference. But the grated fragments would be much more of a muchness, and the cook might easily be deceived by them."

"Then you've thought it was murder all along? You didn't say so yesterday."

"I didn't want you to worry over it."

Lucy thought it was much more likely that her brother had framed his murder theory that very minute, but it was not worth arguing, especially as another point occurred to her.

"Theresa's vegetable grater has been missing since that Saturday. Do you think the murderer could have taken it?"

"That would look like one of the family."

"I suppose it would. I daresay it's just a coincidence. That kitchen's untidy enough for anything to disappear."

"You don't like the idea of it's being Lord Barna then?"

"Of course not. Or Mr. Osmund either. It's unthinkable."

"But unless the maids were lying—"

"Perhaps they were. Ivor suggested," said Lucy, "that the maids might have done it for divilment, meaning to make her sick, but never intending to kill her."

"Is it likely anyone would play such a daft trick?"

"Theresa looks silly enough for anything."

"She does, does she? And how would she have got hold of the monkshood?"

"Through Larry Quin."

"And Larry goes out of his way to indicate to the police where he got it from."

"Yes, to stop them suspecting him."

"He also went out of his way at the inquest to prove that the roots couldn't have got accidentally mixed up on the compost heap. If he's the criminal, he's a supersubtle one."

"Wait though, mightn't the maids have picked the monkshood up in the road? If it was lying under the wall of Beechfield they would be passing that way on Sunday morning, on their way to early Mass."

"But it's much more likely to have been one of the family."

"Why shouldn't it have been Miss FitzEustace? She must have had plenty of opportunities on Sunday morning."

"And Lady Madeleine with her all the time?"

"We've only her own word for that."

"Bunk!" said Linnaeus. "You needn't go dragging Miss FitzEustace in as a red herring. She was only there by chance and there's nothing whatever to connect her with the crime."

"You might give me credit for not being quite so silly as all that," retorted Lucy. "Miss FitzEustace is the one person who was actually seen in possession of the monkshood."

Lucy had told Linnaeus about the monkshood in church, but he had forgotten. He refused to allow it much importance.

"She must have picked it up in the road. If Colonel Murray's right, the fellows who stole the green figs flung it over the wall."

"Yes, but why should she pick it up? Suppose she was on the look out for some means of injuring Lady Madeleine. You can't deny that she fastened on to her that afternoon at Beechfield. I'm convinced she was determined to get the entry to the household."

"That was just a case of business first. You don't collect titled patrons without some boot licking."

"Well, I think she's a little bit dotty. You should have heard Duffy describe how she was muttering to herself when she put the flower stalk into the altar vase. Suppose it was some crazy way of dedicating the deed."

Linnaeus laughed in a way that his sister found infuriating.

"Somewhat farfetched," he commented.

"You can say what you like," Lucy declared, "but I shall ask her the first time I see her, what she was doing with that monkshood."

"She might have wanted it for a spell. Take care she doesn't put a curse on you."

"Funny, aren't you?"

The intellectual standard of the discussion was degenerating, and, in the heat of the argument, Lucy's knitting had taken a wrong turn. She had to take it over to the window and concentrate on it in what was left of the daylight. When she had pulled it back to some rows before the stage at which she had started it that evening, she returned to her chair, and Linnaeus, who did not always realize when one had had enough of something, began again.

"What seems to emerge from your interview this afternoon is that that young man had a money motive."

"Had he?" said Lucy in her most uninterested voice, and went on knitting repressively. But at the end of another row she exclaimed,

"I don't know why it never struck me before. It must have been Mr. Osmund. It must, Linnaeus. Don't you see, it was he who gave out the helpings?"

"What's that got to do with it?"

"Why, because nobody else would have known how to give the monkshood to one person only. If it was Roland, he ran the risk of poisoning Mr. Osmund and Miss FitzEustace too."

Linnaeus got up to let the cat out. Then he got up to let it in again. After this diversion he replied,

"Didn't Osmund say at the inquest that he never took horseradish? His nephew would know that. Or perhaps he didn't mind running the risk. As for Miss FitzEustace, he didn't know she was coming. Whereas, if it was Osmund, he stood by and let Roland help himself. No, as far as that goes, it might have been either of them. They each took care not to poison themselves. If one had got ill it would look worse for the other."

"If they had," said Lucy, "you'd only say the illness of the one was a blind. I know you."

"Then again," said Linnaeus, "there's always the possibility that they collaborated."

"Oh no. They don't get on well enough for that."

"Perhaps that's a blind."

At this point the usually unobtrusive Remus brought himself to their notice by sounds of scurrying and scuffling in a corner. Remus was a middle-aged cat, fond of quietness and given to looking on the milk when it was white, but now and then he had his kittenish aberrations.

"What's Remus playing with?" asked Linnaeus. "Has he got a mouse?"

"I hope it isn't a bird," said Lucy. She stooped down and picked up a small messy object.

"It's a piece of root," she said. "A small piece cut off a tap root." Their eyes met.

"I don't suppose even a botanist could identify it," said Lucy. "But all the same, where would he get a small bit chopped off like that?"

"Did somebody drop it?" asked Linnaeus. "One of our guests last night?"

"Or Miss FitzEustace, when she was here on Monday?"

"Well it's not much good as a clue. Remus has removed anything like fingerprints."

But Lucy stopped herself on the point of throwing it away, and slipped it into the pocket of her cardigan.

"We're not much forrader," remarked Linnaeus. "Unless the police can dig up some more evidence I shouldn't think they could ever pin it on anybody."

Neither of them recognized the fact that, ever since they had heard the first account of the tragedy from Miss FitzEustace, the thread leading to the final, conclusive evidence had been in Lucy's hands.

CHAPTER XV
Tennis and Talk

THE McGOLDRICKS' tennis party, though convened at short notice, was a representative Clonmeen gathering. Nonplayers outnumbered players as women outnumbered men and the old outnumbered the young, but this was usual, and mattered less in Mrs. McGoldrick's view than not to have invited everybody who might hear she had been entertaining.

The tennis players were Dora Cuffe, Mr. Naylor and his two daughters, Colonel Murray, Wendy, Ivor, and the two McGoldrick girls. If Mr. McGoldrick arrived in time (he was expected home for the week end) there would be a men's four.

The different vintages of old ladies might be distinguished by their styles, for externals tend to become fixed at the moment when old age sets in. Old Tallon was a bundle of black (which she had worn ever since her husband was killed in the South African war), with a hat such as one sees on Queen Victoria in late photographs. Young Mrs. Tallon, her daughter-in-law, whose husband was only killed in the last war, was a modern woman of the nineteen-twenties who used a long cigarette holder and still had her hair waved.

Miss Milfoyle, coming somewhere between the two, still managed mysteriously to obtain the kind of flat Edwardian platter that was balanced straight on top of the head, and wore her fox fur as if it was a feather boa. The fixation period, however, could not always be taken as a guide to their age, because Dora Cuffe's Aunt Lottie was of the nineteen-twenties, with a basin-shaped felt hat and short skirts, while her younger sister, Aunt Lettie, always the delicate one, came almost into line with Miss Milfoyle, with a wide shady straw and a great many cashmere silk scarves. If Miss Milfoyle left off her fox fur, even in August, she might get neuralgia; if Aunt Lettie wore one silk scarf too many and got overheated, or one too few and caught cold, she would be very ill and give her sister and niece a great deal of trouble. As for old Mrs.

Tallon, her daughter-in-law faced with resignation the prospect of her being quite knocked up for two days by the excitement of the party. But all these ladies had experienced how very ill one can be without ever dying, though a strong woman like Lady Madeleine seemed to snuff out as readily as the candles on a birthday cake.

Mr. and Mrs. Nichol-Jervis had been invited, but, warned in time by Ivor, had wriggled out. Lucy and Mrs. Naylor, and Miss FitzEustace who had been brought by Miss Milfoyle, sat down resignedly among the old ladies.

The first half-hour passed quickly in arranging deck chairs and wicker chairs, in running in and out with rugs and wraps, in the settling of old Mrs. Tallon, in introducing Miss FitzEustace to everybody she had not met before, and in badinage at the expense of Ivor and Wendy, for it seemed that everyone already knew about the milk cart. Even if the more religious of the two Naylor girls had not been out early to chapel, and Dora Cuffe had not got up before breakfast to gather mushrooms, so that both of them witnessed the dancers' return with their own eyes, the man from the Rosefield dairy would not have missed telling such a good story at all the back doors on his morning round. In all social indiscretions it is the woman who pays. Ivor escaped into the first tennis set, but Wendy, having unwisely confessed to feeling a little tired, had to sit still and suffer all the inevitable jokes about the morning after the night before. Lucy, still harboring remnants of disapproval, felt that the punishment fitted the crime.

Once the party was assembled, Mrs. McGoldrick, from a deck chair in the lee of old Mrs. Tallon, could watch whichever of her daughters happened to be playing and listen to the other one being polite to the old ladies, and congratulate herself in peace. Whatever knocks fate had in store for Mrs. McGoldrick on the morrow, today had all the elements of success.

As for the recent tragedy, every hostess knows what a blessing it is to have something everybody can talk about. The nearness of Annalee Hall enhanced, if anything, the delightfulness of the occasion. Who could look at the gray old house without a shudder? The row of garden chairs was drawn up facing in that direction.

For a wonder, none of the eyes and ears of Clonmeen had yet detected Wendy Nichol-Jervis's engagement to Lord Barna, so nobody but Lucy Bex felt that anything need be left unsaid. And as Lucy could not honestly pretend to be superior to the general curiosity, it was a relief to her finer feelings when the first set ended, and Wendy went to partner Ivor in the second.

Just as everybody at the committee meeting on Wednesday had known about Dunne's, the rumor of murder had got about. There was a murder school of thought and an accident school of thought. Aunt Lettie who, being an invalid, was a great reader, had known all along it was murder, and had somehow never liked Mr. Osmund, while as for Lord Barna, some of those old families had dreadful histories, and wouldn't it be dreadfully sad for such a fine-looking young man? Dear old Miss Milfoyle, rather than think ill of anybody on a higher plane, was sure that it must have been the cook. But young Mrs. Tallon, who always warned you when the milk was not clean and who had exposed the un-hygienic methods of the butcher, knew for certain that there had been several families upset by food coming from Dunne's and assured Lucy that "everybody" was changing their grocer, even if it meant carrying things out from town.

It came as a surprise to the others to find that the Naylors had known Lady Madeleine quite well. As well-to-do sociable Roman Catholics with a growing family, they had a wider orbit than the more retiring widows and spinsters. They went to the races, where they met Lady Madeleine as often as not, and once a month both Mrs. Naylor and Lady Madeleine would travel up to Dublin for the sole purpose of playing bridge at a women's club to which they both belonged.

The attention of the audience wavered between Mrs. Naylor, who had known Lady Madeleine best, and Miss FitzEustace, who had seen her last.

Lucy had, of course, to admit having been with Miss FitzEustace to the inquest. Beyond that, she did not feel inclined to be generous with information or let any suspicion of inside knowledge on her part deter others from telling all they knew. She was not tempted to make a sensation by announcing, for instance, that she had had the gentlemen from the Hall to dinner, and she sincerely hoped Clonmeen would not find out the fact for itself. So she found herself playing a double game in the conversation, and, indeed, behaving little better than a real detective.

"Was Lady Madeleine good at bridge?" she asked Mrs. Naylor. Mrs. Naylor screwed up her face in a deprecating expression.

"So-so, I'd call her. She was too impulsive. Her game was sound enough, but she was a rash bidder. I know that to my cost, as I've never gone down so much in my life as one afternoon when she was my partner. Only last week, too. Dear me, isn't it very sad to think of?"

"Did she play high?" asked Dora Cuffe. Mrs. Naylor replied that the stakes were generally half a crown a hundred, at which all three pairs of Cuffe eyebrows went up. The Miss Cuffes themselves played bridge at least twice a week in the winter, when they could by any means inveigle a neighbor to make a fourth. They would sit up round the card table till all hours, picking up the cards and laying them down again according to ritual, and chatting away as merrily as if the wireless was on. But they never played for money, merely, as they said, for the interest of the game.

"Racing, too," murmured Miss Lottie. "That must have cost her a pretty penny."

"Unless she was lucky," said Miss Lettie.

Mrs. Naylor did not think Lady Madeleine had been particularly lucky. Lucy reflected that bridge and betting losses would explain how poor Roland's bill was left unpaid, and her thoughts also wandered to the day when she had seen Lady Madeleine postdate the check she cashed in Dunne's. But Dora Cuffe was saying she supposed Lady Madeleine had lots of money.

"Look at her lovely clothes!"

"Clothes rationing didn't make much difference to her," said young Mrs. Tallon. "Of course, there's such a thing as getting the use of the maids' coupons."

"Not my maid's," said several voices at once.

"If you ask me," said Mrs. Naylor charitably, "it wasn't so much her clothes at all, as her appearance. In fact, she once told me she believed in spending more, proportionately, on beauty treatments. 'What's the good of being well dressed,' she said to me, `if people look at your clothes and not at you?' "

"Listen to Mammy," muttered Chrissie Naylor to Gwennie McGoldrick. "And she's so mean she won't let me have a facial. Will yours?" Though Chrissie well knew that Gwennie, who was as plain as she herself was fluffy, had never contemplated such an experiment.

Colonel Murray, representing masculine opinion, said he could never understand why women wanted to put so much stuff on their faces, because it deceived nobody. Dora Cuffe's Aunt Lottie said when she saw a gel with makeup on she always wanted to tell her to go and wash her face. But Dora herself showed her independence by declaring that she saw no harm in it and would do it herself, only she just couldn't be bothered.

"It would be wasted on Clonmeen," she said. A fact which none of the Clonmeen people denied.

Lucy was afraid they had got right off the subject of Lady Madeleine, when old Mrs. Tallon, who, at ninety, remembered things that other people had forgotten, remarked,

"Wasn't her ladyship's face valued at a hundred pounds?"

At first nobody knew what she meant. Young Mrs. Tallon asked, "What's that you're saying, Mother?" adding, aside, "She mixes things up, you know." Old Mrs. Tallon in a spirit of tit-for-tat only replied that she was afraid her daughter-in-law was getting a little deaf. It was Miss FitzEustace who came to the rescue, by saying that she thought the old lady referred to the lawsuit against ——'s (naming a well-known Dublin grocer).

"It was in all the papers about five years ago," she said, and several other ladies began to remember having heard something about it at the time. In those days the Osmunds lived in Merrion Square, and Clonmeen had no reason to be interested in them.

By some mischance, there had been washing soda mixed with sugar in the Osmunds' stores. Lady Madeleine had got some of it in her mouth. Luckily she did not swallow any, but it burnt her about the lips, and she sued the grocer who had supplied the goods. Till the case came on, Lady Madeleine went about in a chiffon veil, and her counsel declared in court that she might have been, if not poisoned, permanently disfigured. She was awarded a hundred pounds damages and costs. After the case closed Lady Madeleine unveiled, and her friends were pleased to see that her face was perfectly all right again.

"Unlucky with her grocers, what?" Colonel Murray barked cheerfully. He was an upholder of the accident theory, which this story seemed to him to strengthen.

"Funny, history repeating itself like that," said Miss Lottie Cuffe. Miss Lettie said in a psychic voice that she had always believed coincidences meant something, and sometimes things were sent to warn us. Old Miss Milfoyle wondered if she would ever feel safe again.

Lucy Bex was sitting up as well as she could in her low deck chair, trying to catch Miss FitzEustace's eye. It seemed to her a bit too much of a coincidence, especially when you remembered Norah's evidence at the inquest about finding broken glass in the sugar. Had Lady Madeleine's lawsuit put ideas into somebody's head, and was the sugar incident a first attempt? Or had somebody been trying to murder her from the very first? She really wondered that Miss FitzEustace had never mentioned the washing soda business, which she seemed to have known about all the time. There were so many things she wanted to ask Miss FitzEustace.

But the second set, which everybody had forgotten to watch, came to an end and caused a diversion. Mrs. McGoldrick was concerned at the thought of the court being unoccupied for a moment. There was no sign yet of Mr. McGoldrick, but Gwennie McGoldrick's tennis was considered in Clonmeen the equal of a man's, especially if the man was handicapped by a weak partner like Chrissie Naylor. Ivor and Mr. Naylor had each played two sets, so it fell to Chrissie, Gwennie, Dora Cuffe and Colonel Murray, to be the ones left playing while everybody else went in to tea.

Tea was then announced, and all the lowering of ladies into garden chairs and winding up their legs in rugs and their shoulders in shawls had to be gone through again in reverse. As Lucy and Miss FitzEustace were two of the more mobile guests, the opportunity for a talk had come at last.

They strolled back to the house across the grass, on which two beds of begonias lay like bright thick eiderdown quilts. Behind was a border of salmon pink polyantha roses, and red geraniums filled the two stone bowls at the foot of the house steps. Annalee House, later in date than the Hall and the Lodge, was a red brick square on top of a granite basement, with an unnecessarily imposing flight of steps up to the front door. The red brick glowed and all the mica in the granite winked in the afternoon sun. "Like what you'd see in England," commented Miss FitzEustace, and Lucy knew what she meant. Mown grass and bedding out and general bright tidiness were still their idea of England, as they remembered it before the war.

Lucy knew where she was making for: that corner of the drawing room behind the grand piano, where there was just room for two to stand and the piano to put your cups on. It was a long way from the tea, spread out on a round table in the bay window, but that made for privacy, and Ivor could be depended on to keep them supplied. As soon as they had each laid in tea and tomato sandwiches ("Do take two, they're very small"), Lucy began to fish for Miss FitzEustace's ideas about the mystery.

"Coincidence my eye!" said Miss FitzEustace. "If you'll excuse my vulgar way of putting it. I see you're still taking an interest, Miss Bex.

You were so kind, coming with me the other day. Well now, I'll tell you something, and see what you think."

And what Miss FitzEustace had to tell was nothing less than the true inside story of the washing soda case. She had heard all about it, first hand, from her dressmaker, who had been Lady Madeleine's lady's maid in Merrion Square.

This young woman had seen Lady Madeleine coming out of the pantry one Sunday afternoon. It was remarkable as the only time she had known her ladyship set foot in the kitchen. Some mistresses have a weakness for coming down and trying out little dishes that they make themselves, but not Lady Madeleine. When she wanted to order meals, she sent for the cook to come upstairs. In another mistress this appearance in the basement would have looked suspiciously like snooping, for the cook and housemaid were out, the house-parlormaid was changing her frock, and the lady's maid had no business to take her downstairs just then. But Lady Madeleine, God bless her, was never the sort to look in the pig pail. The house was run on the principle of "lashings and leavings."

It was none of the lady's maid's affairs, but *esprit de corps* made her glance inside the pantry after her ladyship had gone. There did not seem to be anything anybody could complain about: the cold meat was covered and everything was tidy. The only thing was, there were some grains of sugar spilt on the shelf, and the sugar crock was out of place.

It was that same evening at supper that all the fuss began about the washing soda being mixed with the sugar. At first the lady's maid thought nothing of it, but when she heard that Lady Madeleine was getting a hundred pounds damages out of it, she began to wonder if her ladyship had tampered with the stores herself.

The lady's maid was never called as a witness and said nothing of her suspicions at the time. She described herself as one who minded her own business. But five years later, when she had set up on her own as a dressmaker, and Miss FitzEustace was getting a little rayon frock run up for wearing on hot days in Clonmeen, the lady's maid remembered that that was where Lady Madeleine was living now, and there did not seem any harm in gaining a little conversational importance by telling what she knew.

"But how fantastic!" said Lucy. "Fancy anyone burning their own mouth on purpose!"

"Oh yes, she did," said Miss FitzEustace. "I asked her."

"What! You asked Lady Madeleine herself?"

Miss FitzEustace, munching her second sandwich, nodded.

"You mean to say, you actually discussed the matter on that very Sunday morning?"

"No, on Saturday afternoon. What I thought was, if this woman was spreading stories like that about her, Lady Madeleine ought to know."

Lucy was silent in admiration of Miss FitzEustace's nerve. Several avenues for speculation seemed to be opened. Suppose Lady Madeleine had once succeeded in obtaining damages on false pretenses, would she have dared to try it again? Would she have made two attempts (the broken glass being one) with the same shop? Was the monkshood affair an accident in a different sense from what they had imagined, Lady Madeleine having intended to make herself slightly ill and gone too far? That seemed to be Miss FitzEustace's theory. But if she had had such an intention, would she have pursued it, knowing there was some one near at hand who could expose her over the previous incident? And why should she go out of her way to get monkshood of the deadliest variety?

As to that, there was still the problem of just how and when the monkshood had been taken from Beechfield.

Meditating on her earlier cross examination of Duffy, the sexton, Lucy had determined to improve her technique and had mentally rehearsed a way of broaching the subject to Miss FitzEustace. She began by asking if Miss FitzEustace had heard the news of the roots being identified as *Aconitum ferox.* "What I should like to know," said Lucy, embarking on her prepared opening, "what I should like to know is, how did it get into my vase?"

But Miss FitzEustace's eyes were wandering after a large and luscious chocolate cake. "Do you think," she said, "one could secure a piece of that? It looks quite prewar." She was actually moving away toward the tea table when Lucy luckily managed to signal to Ivor. He captured the cake and helped Miss FitzEustace to a large slice, but when she sampled it she looked disappointed.

"Potato flour," she mumbled through crumbs. "Stodgy. Ah well, what can you expect in these days?"

"What I should like to know—" began Lucy again.

"Your nephew," remarked Miss FitzEustace, "is quite the lion of the party. Has he been doing much bombing lately?"

"No. He's on patrols, and lately he's been doing instructor's work. What I should like to know," went on Lucy, feeling like a gramophone needle that has got stuck, "What I should like to know about that monkshood is, who put some of it into my flower arrangement in church? Duffy told me it was some lady he didn't know, and I should have thought Duffy knew everybody."

She looked very hard at Miss FitzEustace, who burst out laughing. "Well, I can tell you that," she replied, without the least concealment. "I brought it there myself."

Lucy feigned astonishment.

"You did, Miss FitzEustace? But what for?"

"Oh, I found it lying in the dust of the road. Don't you hate to see a flower thrown away? So I picked it up and brought it with me to early service. I'm sorry if I upset your flower arrangement, but there didn't seem to be anywhere else to put it. I said to myself, 'the stone which the builder rejected shall become the head of the corner.' "

So that was what Duffy had heard her muttering. Miss FitzEustace was always handy with a scriptural quotation.

"Mind you," said Miss FitzEustace, "I didn't recognize it as that particular monkshood. They all look much the same to me. I see things in color and mass, you know. I'm not a botanist."

"But, Miss FitzEustace, whereabouts on the road did you find it? It might give the Nichol-Jervises a clue to the person who stole their green figs."

This time Miss FitzEustace did look a shade disconcerted.

"If you wouldn't mind, Miss Bex, I'd just as soon you wouldn't mention it to the Nichol-Jervises. It wasn't on the road at all. You see, I was rather late, so I couldn't resist taking a shortcut up the Beechfield avenue, as there was nobody about. But I'd rather the Nichol-Jervises didn't know I'd been so presumptuous, seeing I've only just met them the once."

It seemed as if Miss FitzEustace, at any rate, might be taken off the list of suspects. Looking at her in the innocent enjoyment of her piece of chocolate cake, Lucy felt ashamed of her doubts. She went back over the new information she had received that afternoon, to see if it threw any light on the other persons of the drama.

Suppose it was not Lady Madeleine who had attempted to fake accidental poisoning? Anyone who had known the inside story of the previous case would have felt doubly safe from an accusation of murder. If the substitution of the monkshood for the horseradish did not pass as an accident, then the facts about the washing soda could be brought to light, and everyone would think, as Miss FitzEustace did, that the deceased had fallen a victim to her own scheming. Without going so far as to prove anything, Lucy did think you might say that a person who remembered the washing soda case was more likely to have hit on that particular murder method, and by the same token, a person who knew the true story behind the case was even more probable as a murderer.

"Miss FitzEustace!" said Lucy. "Do you suppose Mr. Osmund or Lord Barna knew what Lady Madeleine was up to over the washing soda affair?"

"I don't know about Lord Barna," replied Miss FitzEustace. "I know Mr. Osmund didn't. As soon as I mentioned it she begged me not to give her away to him, and of course I didn't, not when she was commissioning a picture." She licked the last remains of chocolate icing from her lips and added reflectively, "It's often worth while knowing a little about people beforehand, by way of an introduction."

The artist's manner was so serene that the word "blackmail" never occurred to Lucy till afterwards. Then she did wonder what kind of previous information Miss FitzEustace might have acquired about the Marioffs, Mossbanks, and Gore-Hartys who had patronized her so generously. Perhaps she had not been so far wrong after all when she made Miss FitzEustace out to be a sinister figure.

CHAPTER XVI
Something Else To Think About

THE LAST SET of tennis players had come in to tea and were making up for lost time. The first comers, having finished eating, were talking all the harder. Ivor was kept busy answering questions, explaining to Miss Milfoyle that he had never bombed Berlin, and telling Chrissie Naylor that navigating (which was his function) was quite simple when you knew how.

"You do it by the stars, don't you?" said Chrissie, feeling that he might offer to come out one night and teach her. Gwennie McGoldrick inconsiderately interrupted,

"We heard a Sunderland patrol boat on the wireless. There was a man who kept on saying 'Good shee-ow, chaps!' He sounded just like you."

"There!" exclaimed Wendy Nichol-Jervis, turning round, "I keep on telling him he's got a terrible English accent."

"Well, anyway, it wasn't me. I'm only the fellow who says 'O.K.' "

Lucy had released Miss FitzEustace, but remained in her refuge behind the grand piano, listening to other people's voices. It was hot indoors, even with all the windows open, and it seemed as if Mrs. McGoldrick might think of moving back to the garden. She was trying to get Joan, her other daughter, busy on arranging another set. The chatter dinned in Lucy's ears, when they were distracted by other sounds indicating that Mr. McGoldrick had arrived.

First, a car laboring heavily up to the front door. Then a voice in the hall, "What on earth's all this stuff lying about? My God, is the house full of people?" Next minute Mr. McGoldrick walked in, looking very black-avised thanks to the attentions required by the charcoal engine on his car.

"There you are, Father!" beamed Mrs. McGoldrick.

"Yes," said her husband. "Why didn't you tell me you were having a party? I'd have stayed away. Sorry I can't shake hands with anybody. I suppose you've drunk all the tea."

"I've just sent for some fresh," said Mrs. McGoldrick placidly. "Father, here's Ivor Bex, home on leave again."

Ivor's name had the magical effect of turning Mr. McGoldrick gracious. "Where is he?" he demanded. "Ivor, my fine fellow, I'm delighted to see you. I thought it was only a pack of old women. Proud to shake hands with you," said Mr. McGoldrick heartily, forgetting the blackness of the charcoal. "Listen, you don't want to drink the stuff my wife calls tea nowadays. Come and have a whisky and tell me all about the war."

"Now, Father," protested Mrs. McGoldrick, "you can't take Ivor away from the party. All the girls would be furious with you. Wash your hands now, and when you've had your tea you can put on your flannels and come and make up a men's four."

"Good God! Do you expect me to play tennis in this heat? And after a day like I've been having. It's all right for people who have no work to do. Oh well, Ivor, some other time. Shouldn't have thought this sort of thing was much in your line. Poodle-faking, we used to call it." He suddenly caught sight of the clock, pulled out his watch, and made a dive for the wireless; it was time for the six o'clock news. Next moment all conversation was either "sshed" or drowned. This had the effect of dividing the party. The older people mostly wished to stay and listen, but the younger ones, led by Ivor and Gwennie, seized the opportunity to escape to the tennis court.

Lucy was not over fond of hearing the news, and knew she had a sympathizer in old Miss Milfoyle, who always said she could face things better if she read them in the paper. They slipped away together, Lucy offering Miss Milfoyle her arm for a turn round the garden. They would be each other's excuse to escape from the talk and the tennis and enjoy a peaceful interlude. Lucy felt a healing relief as they turned their backs on the house and the voice of the wireless faded away behind them. She liked Miss Milfoyle, for, if not exciting company, she was never stupid, and was not afraid of silence when she had nothing to say. She could hardly guess that at Miss Milfoyle's gentle hands she would experience the worst shock of the afternoon.

They made their way through a maze of little flower beds packed with annuals inside neat box edgings and down a central path where, to one side, hybrid tea roses, and to the other, sweet peas, were cultivated in extreme perfection. Searching in vain for a greenfly on Mrs. Sam McGredy or Mrs. Van Rossem, counting the sweet pea flowers, six or seven to a stalk, both ladies expressed as much admiration as if Mrs. McGoldrick herself were within earshot. But each knew the other was thinking how much nicer it was to garden by less academic standards. The Bexes often ordered plants on the attraction of their names alone, continually experimented with doubtful doers, and cherished spindly remains of things that had been in their garden before they were born. As for Miss Milfoyle, she could not really get interested in any variety until it was in danger of being lost to cultivation. So they praised the McGoldricks' floristic triumphs without envying them. But when they reached the end of the path, and a turn brought them to a deep border filled with gladioli in all the most delicate shades from rose to apricot, rank after rank of lovely spires just unfolding their largest flowers in a sunset glow, both ladies were at first speechless with astonishment, and then they exclaimed with one voice: "Where ever do they get the manure?"

But though the massed gladioli were spectacular, the McGoldricks' garden was not one to demand close inspection. They walked on down to the end of the border and then turned back, and it was then that Miss Milfoyle said,

"Now that I have got you to myself, Miss Bex, may I be indiscreet? I should like to ask whether we are soon to hear of an engagement?"

Lucy's first thought was that the news about Wendy and Lord Barna had leaked out. She was just going to confirm the rumor and express her hopeful views of the match, when Miss Milfoyle, having noticed her slight hesitation, went on,

"Ivor is a little younger, is he not? You know, I was at both their christenings. But the war has made such a man of him."

"Ivor?" repeated Lucy. "You surely don't expect him to get engaged, Miss Milfoyle, dear. Why, he's still only a boy. Besides, whom could he possibly get engaged to?"

"Well, really, after this morning's romantic little episode—"

"Good gracious, you don't mean Wendy Nichol-Jervis? Oh no, Miss Milfoyle, they are just old friends, nothing more. I do assure you," said Lucy, rather agitatedly, "that there is nothing romantic in the relationship."

"Dear me," said Miss Milfoyle, "I confess I am disappointed. They seemed to me to make a delightful couple. However, I suppose you are the person to know. Though really, to see them together—well, well, times have changed since I was a girl."

"Certainly I ought to know," said Lucy. "They were boy and girl together, and Wendy, has been ordering Ivor round all her life. She is quite two years older than Ivor. I don't expect him to think of marriage for years yet."

"But they do grow up quickly, don't they?" said Miss Milfoyle. "It isn't altogether pleasant for us to see them all ready to take charge of their own lives."

"Oh, as to that," replied Lucy, and she believed what she was saying, "I shall be delighted to see Ivor settle down when he finds the right girl. But it won't be Wendy Nichol-Jervis."

"Well, you sound very sure. Forgive an old woman's curiosity."

Lucy pressed Miss Milfoyle's arm in hers, in acknowledgment of what she knew was a sincere and friendly interest. She said earnestly,

"I should be very sorry to think any such rumor was going round. If you hear anything of the kind, I do beg you to contradict it."

She walked Miss Milfoyle rather rapidly back to the rest of the party. She had been given something to worry about besides detection.

The tennis still continued, but the onlookers were beginning to disperse. Mr. McGoldrick was rather a blight on conversation. His contribution to the topic of the mystery was a tirade on the inefficiency of the Civic Guards.

"Needn't expect those fellows to find out anything. All they're fit for is interfering with the likes of you and me. Can't cut a branch off a tree without having one of them on the doorstep. Spend their lives getting out forms for this and that. Waste of the taxpayer's money. But as for catching a murderer—why, they can't even catch a little boy stealing fruit. Has your father ever heard who took his fig crop, Wendy? No, nor he won't. Call themselves a police force! Ah, they're not the old R.I.C."

Nobody felt like arguing with him. The Tallons, the Cuffes, Miss Milfoyle and Miss FitzEustace said good-bye. The Naylors also tried to go but could not, because, as Mr. McGoldrick had, after all, changed into his flannels, there had to be a men's four. So Lucy, too, sat down again, and Wendy, though looking dead tired, waited with her, while Ivor, Mr. Naylor, Colonel Murray and Mr. McGoldrick played two more sets. Then at last the party came to its fag end.

Wendy was not on her bicycle, as she had a puncture, so she walked back with Lucy and Ivor. As they passed the gate of Annalee Hall she remarked,

"Roland's going back to his flat tonight."

"Is he?" Lucy was surprised.

"Yes. He phoned me at lunch time."

"Wasn't it rather a sudden decision?"

"Oh no. He was going in a day or two anyway." Wendy kicked a stone neatly ahead of her with each foot in turn, then lost it, in the gutter. "He asked me what I thought, and I said I didn't want him to stay on just in order to be near me. I didn't think it was very good for him being all the time with Mr. Osmund."

"Did they have a row?" asked Ivor.

"No, of course not!" Wendy snapped. She was dead tired and on edge. Lucy frowned at Ivor and they walked on in silence. At the gate of Beechfield, Ivor said to Wendy,

"How about tomorrow?"

"I'm lunching with Roland," said Wendy. "Saturday, you know. We'll probably do something or other in the afternoon."

"Right," said Ivor. "I'll call round in the evening."

"Do. If I'm not back you'll be company for Mother."

"And why shouldn't you be back?"

"I don't know. It depends." She relented a little. "I'll try."

"I'll be seeing you," said Ivor firmly.

They said good-bye casually, without touching hands. Lucy added a recommendation to Wendy to go to bed early and have a good night's rest. Then, just as so often when they were children, she took her nephew home.

CHAPTER XVII
Ivor

AFTER DINNER, the three Bexes sat in the garden room. The evening meal had been late on account of the tennis party. Afterwards they had strolled round the garden, which there was only just light to see, and had gathered up enough twigs to indulge in a small summer evening fire. It was pleasant to have everybody satisfied to sit quiet in the firelight, Ivor too tired to be active, Linnaeus as usual nursing the cat. Lucy would have been happier to go on knitting vaguely and feeling harmonious, but she braced herself for an effort.

"Ivor," she said, "I am going to scold you, and I hope your father will back me up."

Ivor could guess what was coming. He replied, in the voice that generally got a rise out of Lucy,

"O.K., Auntie. You kin shoot."

But Lucy disregarded the voice. She said,

"Ivor, do you really feel it necessary to see quite so much of Wendy Nichol-Jervis?"

"Have a heart, Auntie. I haven't seen her at all for six months."

"Last time you were home on leave you didn't live in her pocket all the time."

"What do you mean, in her pocket?"

Lucy spread out her fingers. "All Thursday afternoon, all Thursday night at the dance, then this afternoon—"

"You can't count today. We had millions of chaperons."

"—and you made an engagement for tomorrow evening. It's too often. Isn't it, Linnaeus?"

Linnaeus only murmured, "Don't ask me. You're the expert on these matters."

"You seem to forget," said Lucy, "that Wendy's engaged."

"Oh no," said Ivor. "I'm not allowed to forget it."

"But, Ivor, I don't think you realize how people talk. Everybody in Clonmeen gossips. Miss Milfoyle spoke to me this afternoon."

"About Wendy's engagement?"

"No, indeed. That hasn't got about yet or people would talk. Miss Milfoyle thinks Wendy ought to be engaged to you."

"Sensible woman," said Ivor. "I think so too."

"Ivor!"

He had dropped his cinema twang, the voice of youth and its precaution against being taken too seriously. Speaking as Ivor Bex, for once, and not as Bing Crosby, he declared,

"I mean it, Aunt Lucy. I think Wendy ought to be engaged to me and nobody else. I've told her so. She didn't agree, but she didn't altogether refuse to listen. I'm still hoping to carry my point, but I haven't much time and I've got to work fast."

Lucy gasped. "But, Ivor, I had no idea—neither had Linnaeus—you never told us you cared about her."

"It's been incubating. I didn't intentionally keep you in the dark, but you see things came suddenly to a head. I was surprised myself. But you can take it as official."

"But this is dreadful."

"Why, you like her, and Father likes her. I should have thought you'd be pleased."

"Of course we both like Wendy. It isn't that. It's you that are so young to be thinking about marriage. Don't forget she's two years older than you are."

"I've grown up, Aunt Lucy. One does. And I don't know how much more I've got."

"Ah, don't!" cried Lucy. Steadying her voice she continued, "Don't let that influence you. You mustn't rush into a war marriage."

Linnaeus spoke out of his shadowy corner, "I think you're wrong there, Lucy. If he wants to get married, let him. Might as well face facts."

Lucy changed her ground. She brought out the argument which she had instinctively kept in reserve because it seemed to her unanswerable. "Anyhow, what is the point in all this? Wendy is engaged to Roland."

Ivor said, "Wendy made a mistake."

"Why should you think that? They are engaged, and you have no right to interfere."

"Damn it, Aunt Lucy! It's time somebody interfered. Are you all going to stand by and let Wendy marry a murderer?"

Lucy was brought up short against the point which she kept mentally evading. When she first heard of the engagement, she had liked

Roland well enough to be sincerely pleased. It was only three days since she had been speaking up for him to Mrs. Nichol-Jervis. How quickly the clouds of suspicion had gathered! Only yesterday, when Roland came up the garden, she had been embarrassed more by having entertained suspicions than by having to take them seriously. Yet more and more she was saying to herself, instead of "He can't be guilty," "He can't be guilty because he's engaged to Wendy."

But if she was prejudiced, how much more so was Ivor! She told him so.

"You can't go accusing him like that just out of jealousy."

"I knew you'd say that. I haven't accused him to anyone but you. I certainly haven't to Wendy. I don't know whether she realizes for herself how the evidence is piling up against him."

"Nonsense! What evidence?"

"He's in debt, for one thing."

"And how do you know that?" Lucy had not told Ivor, only Linnaeus, about the identity of the caller of Wednesday night.

"Couple of chaps I met at the dance were telling me about him. Said he owed money right and left. Now he comes into about two hundred a year. Does that give him a motive, or doesn't it?"

"What's two hundred?" said Lucy, whose values had recently become enlarged. "Besides, I happen to know that talk about his debts was ridiculously exaggerated. And anyhow, evidence of a motive isn't evidence of murder."

"Well, he knew all about *Aconitum ferox* and where to get it, and, staying in the house, he had every opportunity to switch the roots."

"All that applies equally to Osmund," Linnaeus pointed out.

"Maybe," said Ivor. "But it was one or other of them."

"Oh, I don't know. There are still other possibilities."

"Will you take a bet, Father?"

"Oh, hush!" Lucy put her hands over her ears. "Anyhow, you two haven't heard the latest developments."

"No, and it's time we did!" exclaimed Ivor. "I saw you with your nose on the trail this afternoon. Come on, Aunt! Tell us what you got out of Miss FitzEustace."

Lucy saw that she was being sidetracked. Nowadays, no matter where a conversation started, it came round sooner or later to amateur detection. She had by no means finished with Ivor. This Ivor-Wendy situation was even more serious than she had imagined. Ivor seemed to be in an intractable frame of mind, nor had Linnaeus given her as much support as she had expected. Perhaps she had better talk to Linnaeus privately. In Ivor's present mood, to say much more might make matters worse. Better leave what she had said to sink in.

She had been intending all along to share her new information with the family, so she said, with a sigh that was partly a yawn,

"Well, see what masculine opinion makes of this."

The family's first reaction was appreciation of the business methods of Miss FitzEustace. Between them, Linnaeus and Ivor made it out a regular racket. So simple, they pointed out, for somebody who stayed weeks at a time in gossipy country districts, first in one house and then in another. It would be like living in a whispering gallery, and any little scandal one might have to repeat would be sure to go down well. In such circles it would be worth paying anything for silence, even over a mere trifle. Miss FitzEustace's prices did not seem unreasonable. Linnaeus pointed out that she had solved one of the blackmailer's problems, as she could always show a reason for her having received a sum of money. Very likely the thing was done quite often, and that accounted for the extraordinary works of art one saw about. It was no use for Lucy to maintain that painting was Miss FitzEustace's real career, though she might, for once, have advanced the cause of art by devious methods. Ivor and Linnaeus preferred to believe that she was an unscrupulous racketeer and professed to admire her all the more.

"She certainly put the screw on Lady Madeleine," Linnaeus declared. "It was pretty obvious there was something behind that sudden craze to have her garden painted. If suicide had been in question, it might have had us wondering about her sanity."

Neither Linnaeus nor Ivor would have anything to do with any theory of accident. The idea of the roots having come from Dunne's was already ruled out. As for an attempt by Lady Madeleine to fake an accidental poisoning, the risk would have been too great. To use *Aconitum ferox* would have both increased the risk and made the accident look less likely. The very fact that she had got away with such a deception once would make her the last person to do such a thing again.

"But what do you make of the broken glass incident?" Lucy asked. "Was it a first attempt?"

"If so," said, Linnaeus, "it surely wasn't a very hopeful one. The glass was easily spotted, apparently, and it was hardly likely to have killed her."

"Yes, that's what I thought. My idea was that it might have been a try-on by the maids. I don't mean anything like murder, I mean, a try-on to see what they could get out of Dunne's."

"Was Norah there at the time of the washing soda?"

"Yes. Norah's an heirloom. She's been with Lady Madeleine's family for years."

"Was Roland?" asked Ivor.

"I suppose he was."

After a pause, Linnaeus said, "Another point that emerges is that about the monkshood having been found on the drive. If it wasn't lying about in the road, it wouldn't have been picked up by the maids on their way to Mass. What's more, it doesn't look as if it had any connection with the fruit thieves. Their line of retreat would have been over the garden wall."

Lucy reminded him of the tar. "When they found that, they'd go back some other way."

"To get on the drive they'd have had to pass right under the house windows. No, but I can think of a much more likely way for those roots to have gone from Beechfield to Annalee Hall."

"Do you want us to ask you how?"

"What about that basket of plants?"

"Then the Osmunds—?"

"Carried it home themselves. Exactly."

"But we still don't know," said Lucy, "which of them put the plant into the basket."

"Well now," said Linnaeus in a businesslike voice, "we've been doing a lot of guessing. Let's drop the inferences and conjectures and see what we have in the way of facts." (First finger up.) "Somebody obtained the monkshood from Beechfield on Saturday evening, or at night." (Second finger.) "They grated it up some time between then and lunch time on Sunday, probably using the grater that was missing from the kitchen on Sunday morning." (Third finger.) "They substituted the grated monkshood for the grated horseradish. Now, that was most likely done after the horseradish was arranged round the beef on the serving dish."

"Why?"

"Because the murderer didn't throw out the whole of the horseradish. He wanted some of it to be safe. If he put it on the dish himself he could keep the monkshood together in a heap. If you grant that point, it suggests that the substitution was done fairly late on Sunday morning, and that tells in favor of Lord Barna."

"Why yes, of course," cried Lucy. "Roland was late for lunch. He couldn't have done any juggling with the dishes."

"Probably faking an alibi," said Ivor.

Lucy jumped to her feet. "I simply will not go on arguing about it. Ivor, you may think what you like, but you won't convince me that Roland is capable of murder. Nor have you convinced me that Wendy doesn't care for him."

Ivor stood up too. "Never mind, Auntie. Give me time."

Linnaeus did not move. "I've nearly convinced myself," he announced, "that murder was done by one or other of those gentlemen. Lucy, do you have to keep going to Annalee Hall?"

Lucy said, "I wish I might never set foot in it again. But I must look in tomorrow morning to make sure that Mr. Osmund has meals for the weekend. Don't you see how dreadful it is, if he didn't do anything? All this terrible suspicion added to his loss and grief! I must go on helping him if I can. Even the law says a man is innocent until he's proved guilty."

She kissed them both good night. With Linnaeus it was the usual perfunctory parting, but Ivor's hug was an extra, and Lucy guessed that it was a kind of makeweight to balance the part of himself that had passed from her to Wendy. Its effect was rather the opposite to what he intended, for she went to bed uncomforted.

CHAPTER XVIII
The Police Are Not Idle

WHEN LUCY APPROACHED Annalee Hall next morning, she was surprised to hear somebody singing in the kitchen. It was Theresa, returned to duty and evidently making the best of it. She explained that she had gone home for a few days to recover her nerves after all she had gone through, but came back as soon as she felt fit for work, because she knew they would not be managing very well without her. Lucy accepted this at its face value, but if she had known how Theresa's conscience had been stimulated by police inquiries and a scolding from her mother, it would not have surprised her. Theresa, however, had honestly convinced herself that she had come back entirely out of consideration for her employer, and she fairly glowed with virtue.

Theresa seemed quite competent to do the catering and shopping; indeed, there was nothing she liked better than a morning stroll round the shops. So Lucy gladly handed back all responsibility for the domestic affairs of Annalee Hall. But before she could get quite away Norah reminded her of a detail still to be attended to. She had not done anything about the blocked-up handbasin upstairs.

"Oh dear, how stupid of me," said Lucy. "I quite forgot. Suppose we go up and look at it now."

"If you please, ma'am."

Norah led the way up to the big front room where, less than a week ago, Lady Madeleine had died. Lucy could not enter it without a shiver, though it was flooded with sunshine. In one way it was less depressing than the sitting-room downstairs, because all personal possessions had already been removed. But the bareness of the empty dressing-table and the two dismantled beds spoke of the emptiness after death.

Norah, though as dour as ever, did not seem to feel the impression. Her only comment was, "Mr. Osmund might be wanting to sleep here again, now the room's been turned out." She walked over to the washbasin fixture. There was only one, installed by former owners of Annalee Hall who did not use this as a double room. It was an ornate Victorian patent with a blue flowered pattern all over it that did not correspond with the unornamented, up-to-date wallpaper, or the straight divan beds.

The basin was empty and clean. Norah explained that water would still trickle away, but slowly and with reluctant gurglings. She demonstrated.

"Yes, I see," said Lucy. "I think all we have to do is to unscrew something underneath. Couldn't Larry Quin—?"

Norah's expression reminded her that there was a quarrel between her and Larry. She saw she had better not ask the impossible.

"All right," she promised weakly. "I'll bring my nephew round later and he'll fix it for you."

"Thank you very much, madam. I couldn't trouble Mr. Osmund, and his lordship has gone back to town."

"Oh yes," murmured Lucy. "Well, Norah, I'll get it seen to."

But it seemed that the handbasin was not Norah's real worry, merely a pretext for a private interview. The housemaid made no move to go. Lucy wondered when she was coming to the point.

"Could I speak to you, madam?" said Norah suddenly. The formula, coming in the middle of the conversation, clearly introduced a more important theme.

"It's the police, madam," Norah burst out. "I mean, the Guards. They'd have you distracted, showing them this, that and the other, and answering questions morning, noon and night. Whatever you say, you can't please them. What I wanted to ask you, madam, is whether I done right to give them a pair of his lordship's trousers."

"His trousers!"

"Yes, madam. The gray flannels."

"But whatever did they want those for?"

"He didn't say, madam. But he give off to me for cleaning them. It was his lordship himself give them me to clean a-Wednesda'. That was the day of the funeral, and when Mr. Osmund and his lordship were out, a Guard came and went through all the clothes in the cupboards, but these gray flannels was down here at the time. So then, a-Thursda' morning, just after you'd left, madam, the same Guard as was here a-Wednesda' come into the kitchen, and says he, 'What are you doing there?' and says I, 'I was just going to take a bit of tar off of these with turpentine.' And says he, 'You'll do nothing of the sort. I'll take charge of these,' says he, 'and don't you say anything to your master till I give the word. Don't forget now,' he says to me. 'If you tell anybody I took these, I'll have your life.' So what ought I to do, madam?"

Lucy frowned. This reminder of the official investigations was disagreeable. She had supposed vaguely that some kind of inquiry was going on, but so far the police had been remarkably unobtrusive, and neither Mr. Osmund nor Lord Barna had particularly complained. Yet now she learned that all the time there had been coming and going, questioning the servants, turning out drawers and cupboards. And they had found clues, too. One day they had gone off with the book on *Poisonous Plants*, and another with a pair of trousers, but who could imagine what they would make of them?

Lucy remembered seeing the trousers in the kitchen on her first visit, but whatever there was about them that seemed important to the police, was not apparent to her. It must be something to do with the tar on the wall of Beechfield. Did the police not know about the monkshood being found on the drive? Not that it made any difference if it was a case of incriminating Lord Barna; he could have got the roots out either way Suppose he had climbed that wall on Saturday night? Lucy wished she had a more legal notion of what constituted evidence, but in common sense she did not see how the tar could prove anything.

"What ought you to do, Norah?" she repeated, coming out of her abstraction. "Well, we all have to do what the police say. I don't suppose you ought to have told me, even, but probably I wouldn't count. Did Lord Barna ask you for the trousers?"

"Yes, madam, he did, when he was packing. So I said to him that I hadn't cleaned them yet, which was telling him no lie. But he'll be expecting me to post them on to him."

"I daresay the Guards will return them soon."

"I hope so, I'm sure," replied Norah skeptically. "But what does it mean, madam?"

"I don't know any more than you do, Norah."

Norah muttered, looking at the floor. "I'm sure I never thought to see myself mixed up with murder."

People have a peculiar instinct to hush up disasters and scandals before children and domestics, who, however, generally know more of the real facts than anybody else. Lucy said to Norah, speaking very clearly and kindly, that she must not go imagining things, because of course it could not have been anything but a very sad accident. "Who could possibly want to murder a lady like your mistress?"

But Norah wagged her head at that. "I wouldn't care to say, madam. Some families is different when you see them in their own houses."

"But you had stayed with her a long time, hadn't you?"

"Five years, madam, and fifteen with the old lord. I don't say I'd anything to complain of myself, but I see what went on. She had enemies."

Ladies, Lucy reflected, do not listen to servants' gossip. But amateur detectives sift evidence to the bottom. She folded her arms and gave Norah a piercing look.

"Norah, have you any special reason to say that?"

"I wouldn't care to say, madam."

"You had better be careful, you know. Did her ladyship," (Lucy knew this was an unscrupulous suggestion, but she had to make it) "did her ladyship ever say she thought that someone was trying to poison her?"

Norah shook her head. "Oh no, madam, nothing like that."

"What about the time she found broken glass in the sugar?"

"But she didn't—" Norah broke off short and turned slowly red.

Up to now, Lucy suspected, Norah had been lugubriously enjoying herself, dropping dark hints, making Miss Bex's flesh creep, and waiting, with the easy reliance of her class, to have her thinking done for her. But the question about the glass seemed to have struck a nerve. Her eyes shifted from Lucy to the door, and she wriggled sideways as if to go.

"Just a minute, Norah," said Lucy. "About that broken glass. Do you mean, her ladyship didn't know?"

"No, madam. She didn't."

"Then who did? Just you and Theresa?"

"Sure the broken glass was neither here nor there," cried Norah, getting angry. "Nobody need have said anything about that, if it wasn't for Larry Quin that would do anything rather than mind his own business. Wasting the gentlemen's time at the inquest. Just out to make trouble."

Lucy looked at her. "There was something fishy, then, about that broken glass. It didn't really come from the shop, did it? Somebody put it among the sugar, to see what they could get out of Dunne's. Somebody who had been with Lady Madeleine at the time of her lawsuit, and knew about her getting damages, and thought they would fake a claim for compensation on their own account. That would lay them open to a charge of obtaining money under false pretenses."

"It wasn't money," said Norah. "Only a little extra sugar."

"It was very wrong of you, Norah." Norah scowled at the floor. Lucy, having found out what she wanted, thought she might allow herself to be more reassuring. There had been harm enough done to Dunne's reputation, but it might not help to stir the matter up again when it would otherwise be forgotten. So she said in her chilliest voice,

"Well, it's nothing to do with me. But I shouldn't advise you to go round talking to people and hinting things, the way you did this morning. You just leave the police to do their own job, and don't you start getting fancies."

"No, madam," said Norah. After a pause she added grudgingly, "Thank you, madam."

"And be careful what you say to Theresa. A silly young girl is so apt to get ideas into her head."

Norah took any criticism of Theresa as an implied compliment to herself. She brightened a little, and said in a condescending tone,

"Ah, she's nothing but a 'go-day, come-day, God send Sunday.' "

In corroboration of this description, Norah added that Theresa had found the vegetable grater in the knife box, and must have put it there herself, instead of in the table drawer where it was usually kept. Lucy thought it strange that Norah should have missed seeing it in a place she must continually have been taking knives from, but then it turned out that the knives the family were using had, between washing up and the next meal, been dumped on the service lift where they would be handy, and were never put right away. In that kitchen, an object was not necessarily lost because it did not immediately come to hand, so it seemed too much to assume that the grater had ever really disappeared at all.

Lucy walked rapidly back by way of the shortcut, intending to hale Ivor over to Annalee Hall at once and set him to work on the handbasin, so that she could be shut of the place. She had left him in the garden. He had come down to breakfast that morning, and afterwards had seemed rather at a loose end.

In the old days, Lucy's nephew had never seemed to be on her hands. As a boy he was always able to find something to do, even if it was only stopping all the clocks and putting them in order again. Besides, in those days, he knew how to do nothing, the art of dawdling, that suits the Irish climate. But since he went to England he had got out of the habit. He was as restless as a dog wanting to be exercised.

Brooding on change, Lucy's heart went out to the rowan, the manure heaps, the pump and the old-fashioned watering-can, representatives of stability. What had the war done to Ivor? Was it responsible for this change in his relations with Wendy Nichol-Jervis? She could not regard that as a natural development. For years and years, Wendy had never let Ivor forget that she was the older child, and entitled to order him around. Ivor's place was two steps lower down on the moving staircase of years, and to run up a moving staircase is cheating.

When it came to comparing her nephew with Lord Barna, Lucy flattered herself that she could see them both without prejudice. Ivor's charm for her was that of being a new edition of the Bexes, and of sometimes looking so like Linnaeus, and sometimes reacting so satisfyingly like herself. But if he belonged in some other family, she fancied she would consider him a fairly commonplace young man. Whereas with Lord Barna, it was quite an adventure if he opened a door for you, and you never knew when he might pay you a compliment. With his looks and his poise, and his nice sensitiveness to one's moods, and his novelty, and the glamor of his misfortunes, she did not see how Wendy could hesitate.

But Lord Barna would have to be innocent, or what would Wendy do? But if it was not Lord Barna, then it was Mr. Osmund who read up the properties of poisonous plants and watched for an opportunity of putting monkshood roots on the dinner table, and planned how the blame would fall on the grocer, and then spoilt that plan by pouncing on the rare and extra deadly variety of monkshood with which the devil, or Providence, tempted him. For the choice between murder and accident hung on the use of *Aconitum ferox*, and one could moralize about the way the murderer, trying to make extra sure, betrayed his hand. But he still had not betrayed who he was: there was no knowing which of the two men was capable of that ingenious, odious plot. Poor Mr. Osmund had nobody to fall in love with him, but one could not condemn him on that account. So what? Lucy was beginning to feel that any solution, however painful to Wendy, would be better than not knowing what to think.

Ten minutes later she had changed her mind. Too absorbed to notice bird songs or voices, she had passed along the wall, through the fence, across the paddock, and had pushed open the back door to her own garden. She found Ivor still there, but not alone. He was sitting on the seat under the apple tree, with his arm round Wendy Nichol-Jervis.

When they heard Lucy come in, they jumped up and came to meet her without embarrassment, and she saw that Wendy was crying. Ivor stood behind her, signaling a warning. He said,

"Wendy has some bad news, Aunt Lucy. She's just heard that Roland has been arrested."

CHAPTER XIX
Arrest

THEY HAD NOT often seen Wendy in trouble, and never anything so shattering as this. The last time Lucy had seen her cry was when her brother, Peter, left for abroad, but they had had time to get used to the idea of that, and besides, it was all in the day's work. This was an out-of-the-ordinary blow. There are routine ways of dealing with the common run of troubles, but in the present predicament a complete ignorance of police methods, and of what might lie before them in the way of criminal proceedings, made the prospect seem even darker than perhaps it really was.

Lucy put all the sympathy she could into her tone of voice and the pressure of her hand and led Wendy back to the seat. The child began being brave at once.

"They won't keep him long," she declared. "They'll find it was a mistake. He's the last person in the world—"

"What have they got against him?" asked Lucy.

"I don't know. I can't imagine. But, whatever it is, I'm sure he'll be able to explain. When you know Roland, the whole thing's so absurd. It's really rather funny." She began to laugh hysterically.

"Be quiet!" said Lucy sharply. "Let me think." What she thought first was that the kitchen fire was out till dinner time. How the fuel shortage did complicate first aid or hospitality! "Ivor!" she said. "Go and put a match to the sticks in the garden room and put just three cupfuls of water in the black kettle, and when it boils make us a pot of real tea. Take some of the tea you brought me, it's in the blue canister in my writing-desk, and the keys are in my overall pocket, and my overall is hanging up behind my bedroom door." Ivor walked off looking capable, and Lucy said the women would sit quietly under the apple tree till tea was ready, and settle what had to be done. She was out to set an example of being very calm and practical.

She inquired how Wendy's parents had received the news.

"Father was out," said Wendy, wiping her eyes. "I haven't told mother yet." Lucy understood the Beechfield tradition that, whatever happened, Mrs. Nichol-Jervis was not to be upset. Besides, she detected in Wendy's faintly defensive tone an awareness of her mother's general disapproval of her fiancé. Wendy said simply,

"I came straight round here to Ivor."

Now that was touching. But, though not behindhand in respect for her nephew's sagacity, Lucy did not see that he could be much help at present.

"A solicitor," she said. "That's what Roland ought to have. I expect he knows that himself. Will they let you see him?"

"I don't know," said Wendy. "I hardly know anything yet. A friend of Roland's, a girl who has a flat in the same house, rang me up about half an hour ago and said he'd been taken away this morning. He asked her to let me know. Two men took him away in a cab. I don't even know where. Would it be Mountjoy, or the Castle, or what?"

Lucy did not know either, so that was one thing they would have to find out. She suggested that it would be best to get in touch with Mr. Osmund.

"Yes, I suppose so." Wendy sounded reluctant. "I wish I knew him a bit better. He's not very approachable, is he?"

"I don't see why you say that."

"Well, I'm going by Roland, you see. I think Roland was a bit afraid of him, at least, I mean, afraid of irritating him. He had a feeling that Mr. Osmund didn't much like him. Roland's so sensitive." Wendy's voice wavered, but she made an effort and pulled herself together. "But it would be silly to mind that now. Could I ring up Mr. Osmund from here?"

"Of course," said Lucy. "You know where the phone is."

They went up to the house together and in by the garden room, where the tea making was just coming to a successful conclusion. Lucy and Ivor waited, letting the tea draw, while Wendy telephoned. But when she rejoined them she had not succeeded in getting through to Mr. Osmund.

"I got his office," she said, "but they wouldn't put me through to him. I gave them my name, because I thought he would come if he knew it was me, but they stuck to it that he was engaged."

"Quite likely he really was," said Lucy. "You'll have to try again later." Wendy did try again after they had all drunk their tea, but with no better luck.

"This time they were quite rude about it," she told Lucy.

"They must all be in such a state over this."

"But what am I to do? Ring him up again? It doesn't seem very much use." Wendy looked hurt and puzzled. "It's quite the hardest thing to have to sit round waiting."

"All right," said Ivor. "Let's go to the police."

The police barracks at Clonmeen was not a place that had any attraction for visitors. Lucy had been there before, to get her kerosene ration card, or to apply for permission to cut a tree. She always found the place made her nervous. The Guards seemed to be different every time. Perhaps it was because they changed so often that the barracks remained so unhomely, and none of them had made much of a success of the garden.

You went through a narrow doorway into a bare room decorated with one recruiting poster and furnished with a desk and some hard chairs.

A Guard sitting at the desk looked, if possible, more official with his cap off. Only a smell of cabbage cooking for the barracks dinner did something to make the atmosphere more human.

The Guard, however, was polite and gave them chairs. He said they had better see the Sergeant, who would be in any moment. Then he went on filling out or sorting out a ream of official forms, and looked so busy that the intruders did not like to make conversation. Time passed. There was nothing to look at, but plenty to think about. Wendy thought about how Roland was getting on in prison. Ivor thought about how Wendy was taking it. Lucy thought about Roland and Mr. Osmund and Lady Madeleine, and the details of that Sunday morning, and all the various disconnected incidents bearing on the affairs of Annalee Hall. And suddenly, whether it was the schoolroom atmosphere, or the pressure of anxiety, or the end of a natural ripening process, all these vegetating thoughts of Lucy's bore fruit and she had what looked to her a good idea.

They had been sitting there for about twenty minutes when Sergeant Dunphy came in, a genial man, with something fatherly, or perhaps more episcopal, in his manner. He knew who they were and guessed they had come in connection with the mystery. But when Lucy spoke of Lord Barna's being arrested, he became enigmatic.

"Who told you that?" he asked.

"Isn't it true?" cried Wendy.

"You can't believe all you hear," replied the Sergeant. "Maybe we're not always as black as we're painted. It's this way, d'you see. Your friend has gone along to the Castle to answer one or two questions. That's a different thing from if he's committed for trial."

"Then he's going to be let out again?"

The Sergeant raised a hand as if to hold up traffic.

"Now as to that, I can't say. It all depends what way things go. If he wasn't able to answer the questions in a satisfactory way, then I don't say but what they might have to commit him for trial after all."

"But if he explains everything?"

"If they don't find enough grounds to commit him for trial," said the Sergeant, "they have to release him within twenty-four hours."

The Bexes glanced at each other, wondering whether this, after all, amounted to much, or whether the Sergeant was only trying to radiate reassurance, like a doctor who tells you that the patient is "extremely comfortable." But Wendy was looking happier.

"Then there's nothing to worry about," she said. "And nothing I can do for him at the moment?"

The Sergeant shook his head. "You just go home and wait till he rings you up."

He might have given her a present, she thanked him so warmly. She slipped her arm through Ivor's and they escaped into the sunshine.

But Lucy lingered behind. Her good idea might be useful or might be merely silly, but she thought it worth a trial. In case it turned out to be silly, it would be premature to let the children know, nor did she care to try it on the Sergeant, but she asked him diffidently,

"Would it be possible to see the detective who is in charge of the case? I think I have some information for him."

The Sergeant told her to see Detective-Inspector Lancey, whom she remembered at the inquest. It would mean going in to the headquarters of the Detective Branch, at Dublin Castle. He would be there that afternoon, and, if she liked, the Sergeant would ring him up and ask him to expect her.

Lucy had meant to spend that afternoon bottling the tomatoes, but she saw that it would have to be put off yet again.

"Is it some information of importance?" asked the Sergeant curiously.

Lucy shrugged her shoulders. "I don't know," she answered primly. "That will be for Inspector Lancey to say."

CHAPTER XX
Interviewing a Detective

THERE ARE STILL those for whom Dublin Castle has associations with the balls and stylishness of the old Ascendancy days. Lucy was not old enough for that, and on this, her first visit, she found the old museum-cum-dungeon as intimidating as its original builders could have hoped.

Ivor had taken Wendy back to Beechfield. He was going to stand by while the news was broken to Mr. and Mrs. Nichol-Jervis, and then he would keep Wendy playing tennis the whole afternoon. So it had not been difficult for Lucy to slip away after lunch and catch the first afternoon bus to Dublin. She rejected Linnaeus's offer to come with her, partly to spare him the sacrifice of a Saturday afternoon, but chiefly because she was not at all sure that she was not going to make a fool of herself, and she preferred to do it without witnesses.

So here she was, after an hour in the packed bus, a little faint, very hot and shiny, and still wincing from walking across some cobblestones, trying to shape her idea into a coherent form in which to get it across to Inspector Lancey. The Inspector was a courteous man, like a long-suffering schoolmaster who expects people to waste his time. It took determination to tackle him, but Lucy reminded herself how nice Mr. O'Gallchobhair had been about the Flower Show, and tried to believe that nearly everybody was human if you got to know them.

Inspector Lancey selected some papers from a folder and patted them into a neat packet. "Well now, Miss Bex," he began, "do you tell me you have got on to something you think our men have overlooked?"

"It's something they couldn't have known about," explained Lucy.

"They're very thorough, you know."

"Oh yes, I know. I heard all about the search they made at Annalee Hall."

"Just routine," murmured the Inspector automatically.

"And about them taking away the book. By the way, I don't know how long fingerprints last, but if that was what you were looking for, you might have found some of my brother's or mine."

"Oh? How's that?"

Lucy told him the past history of the Osmunds' copy of *Poisonous Plants*. Inspector Lancey did not seem particularly interested, but when she had finished he pulled open a drawer in the table at which they were sitting and took a book out.

"Would this be your book, now?" he asked. "Oh, you can handle it, all right. The experts have been over it."

Lucy picked it up, turned over the pages, and identified it as their copy. "I didn't recognize it at first," she said. "It used not to have a brown paper cover on it."

"Did it not, so? Then it must have been put on since." Lucy thought you hardly needed a detective's training to deduce that much. She said,

"Then you did examine it for fingerprints."

"Just routine," said the Inspector. "We only found one lot, though. I mean, we only found several sets from one person."

"And that was?"

"His lordship the Earl of Barna."

He jerked his head slightly, which Lucy took to indicate that Roland was somewhere about, in some other room of this gloomy, grimy building. She wondered if he was under lock and key and whether he knew she was here. She had not asked to see him—there was nothing he could tell her—but she wanted to find out all she could about the case against him. The Inspector did not seem to mind her asking questions. She asked, "Was that why you arrested him?"

"Partly that," said the Inspector. Lucy looked expectant, but he did not open up any further. So she fished again.

"I couldn't imagine," she said, "what you were going to prove with that pair of trousers."

The Inspector frowned, and Lucy wondered for a wild moment—Irish officialdom is so modest—whether she ought to have referred to them as "garments" or "unmentionables." Then she remembered that Norah was not supposed to have told about the trousers, but it did not worry her much if she had got Norah into hot water.

"It was the tar, I suppose," she went on. "I daresay you thought it came from the wall at Beechfield."

"We know it did." The Inspector shuffled his handful of documents and laid one in front of her. "Since you're interested, here's a report from Kilmainham—our Technical Bureau, you know—on the garments in question. It's amazing what those fellows can prove. They say *de minimis non carat lex,* but above there at Kilmainham it's the tiny things that count. They found dust in those tar stains, now, and they analyzed the dust, and made it out to be fragments of stone and mortar identical with a sample from the wall."

Lucy was not scientific minded, she left that to Linnaeus. She was more impressed by the Inspector's Latin than by the experts' results. She said, "That's very clever of them, but would you call it conclusive? Surely all the walls round our way are the same."

"They haven't all been freshly tarred. Oh, I know yours has, for one, but I think that wasn't till Monday morning?" Lucy wondered how he knew that. He was beginning to give her the creeps. "By a coincidence, Miss Milfoyle and the McGoldricks did just the same."

"Yes, and there's another place," cried Lucy, as a thought struck her. "The shrubbery at Annalee Hall itself. They've been cutting branches there and tarring the stumps. Wait, Inspector! I know what you're going to say. But the tarring would have been done by Larry Quin, and if Larry borrowed the tar from his father at Beechfield there might be bits of dust and mortar left on the brush."

"Ingenious," said the Inspector kindly, "but I don't know that it matters, seeing his lordship admits he did climb that wall on Saturday night."

How often Lucy had wished that she could help looking exactly what she felt! She knew from the Inspector's smile how her face had fallen.

"He climbed the wall!" she repeated blankly. "Whatever for?"

"Well," said Inspector Lancey, "I don't know that I ought to tell you that. Maybe you'll be kind enough to treat it as a confidence. He climbed the wall and stole the figs, acting, he says, on Miss Nichol-Jervis's suggestion. Miss Nichol-Jervis feared that the large crop might be dangerous to her father's digestion."

The Inspector's smile had broadened. He was certainly beginning to thaw a little. Either his recent score over Lucy had put him in a good humor, or he was simply getting more accustomed to female society, for even a detective may be a shy man. Lucy's spirits rallied. She was amused at this revelation.

"So it was them," she said. "The creatures! What naughty children they are!"

"It might be as well," suggested the Inspector, "if Mr. Nichol-Jervis did not learn the true facts of the case."

"I'm so glad you aren't going to give them away," said Lucy, momentarily forgetting that anything worse hung over them than the wrath of Wendy's father. She added, "After all, the tar isn't of much importance, is it? I happen to know that the monkshood was found on the drive at Beechfield on Sunday morning. So that looks as if the person who took it never climbed the wall at all."

This time the Inspector did seem mildly interested. He inquired how she knew, and Lucy told him about Miss FitzEustace. He shook his head. "That's a lady who never seemed to be quite open with us," he remarked. "Now that's the kind of thing we're always up against. If people would only come and tell the police what they knew. Not that it matters much in this case. We were never particularly interested in proving anything from the tar."

Lucy stared at him and thought, "Then what on earth have we been talking about all this time?" She began to think the Inspector was playing cat and mouse.

"No, it wasn't the tar," said the Inspector. "The tar didn't interest us so much as what we found in the turn-ups. It's extraordinary what those fellows above in Kilmainham can find in turn-ups. Now the ladies are taking to wearing slacks, that's something for them to think about. It's like down the sides of armchairs, that's another place it's always well worth looking for evidence." Lucy thought that in another half-minute she would scream. "What we found in his lordship's turn-ups, now," concluded the Inspector, "was a piece of monkshood root."

Lucy's heart sank. She saw the evidence piling up against Roland. She wondered how she was ever going to explain what she had come for. It did not seem easy to lead up to her big idea. Not that it seemed such a big idea, after all. It was only the most tenuous of clues, and the Inspector was evidently a man who dealt in hard facts.

At any rate there was no point in concealing anything, and she thought she saw a way to earn the Inspector's good opinion. She felt in her jacket pocket for the bit of root that she had taken from Remus.

"Was it like this?" she asked.

Too cautious to be definite, the Inspector thought it might be. He did not seem to think much of it, but having heard all about it, said kindly it might be an "indication."

"Well, thanks very much, Miss Bex, for dropping in," said Inspector Lancey. "We're always glad to listen to anybody who can give us any information." He gathered up all his papers again, and stood up, holding out his hand. Lucy automatically stood up too, and shook hands with him. Then she recovered her wits.

"Oh but, please!" she exclaimed. "Don't go away. That wasn't what I came in to tell you."

"Something else, is there?" The Inspector paused, a hand on the back of his chair. Lucy gripped her own chair with both hands and faced him across the table.

"It isn't exactly evidence," she explained apologetically, "it's only an idea of mine. There might not be anything in it, but you did say, didn't you, that it was the tiny things that counted? What you've just been telling me, about the fingerprints and the monkshood fragments in his trouser turn-ups, doesn't seem to me to absolutely prove anything against Lord Barna. But I believe I can put you in the way of finding definite evidence against somebody else."

The Inspector waited.

Lucy drew breath, and then explained her share in the management of Annalee Hall during the past week. "So you see, Inspector, I've had opportunities of noticing things. It's second nature, when you're used to all the tiresome little details of housekeeping. So I did think it might be worth while to draw your attention to the blocked up wastepipe in the bedroom handbasin."

"Is the bedroom wastepipe blocked?" asked the Inspector, looking both vexed and puzzled. "They shouldn't have missed a thing like that."

"Oh, you mustn't blame your men. It's not completely blocked, so there's nothing to show unless you run the water. But there is some obstruction. And Norah tells me it wasn't blocked at all when she did the room out on Sunday morning. Norah asked me to get it attended to, you see, and I was going to bring my nephew round this morning. But then I thought about it some more, and it seemed to me that perhaps you ought to look into it."

"We'll look into it, all right," promised the Inspector. "You did quite right to come to us. Sit down again, won't you, Miss Bex, and tell me just what it is you're getting at."

CHAPTER XXI
An Impersonation

LUCY THOUGHT the Inspector would set off for Annalee Hall at once, but he did not share her impatience.

"We want to go about this quietly," he explained. "It's a pity, now, you didn't come to us on a weekday, when the occupier would be at his office. What we want is to drop round there some time when we needn't disturb Mr. Osmund at all. Do you know, is he a churchgoer?"

"I'm afraid not."

"Ah, that's a pity," said the Inspector, with a moral shake of his head. "Well, well, we'll think of something else. He's been asking if he can have an interview with the prisoner. It can do no harm to let him come in here tomorrow morning. That'll give me a chance to send up a couple of men when there's only the maids in the house."

"Not till tomorrow?" said Lucy, disappointed.

"Wait now," said the Inspector, disregarding interruptions. "Here's another idea. You told the housemaid you'd be bringing your nephew round?"

"Yes."

"And does she, or does either of the two maids up there, know this nephew of yours?"

"I shouldn't think so. Ivor's only just come home, and he's never been at the Hall."

"Then here's what I suggest. I'll send a plainclothes man over to your place tomorrow morning. I'll get hold of some fellow who hasn't been up there before. You go round with him to the Hall and let them take him for your nephew, and they won't know the police have a finger in it at all."

"But they'd be sure to guess," said Lucy, trying not to laugh. She did not believe a policeman posing as Ivor would take in Norah or Theresa for one moment.

But the Inspector liked his own way of doing things, devious though it might seem. "If they do guess," he replied, "there's no great harm. Our men have been round there often enough. But it would be just as well if they didn't guess. You don't need to tell them it's your nephew. Just say what you've come for and let them draw their own conclusions."

Lucy still did not think much of the idea, but the Inspector apparently did not require her to lie right out, so she agreed to do as she was told. "But don't blame me if anything goes wrong. And, of course, it may all be a wild goose chase."

"We'll take the risk of that," said the Inspector.

So Lucy went home, ridden by a sense of responsibility, and apprehensive about the morrow. She did wish her theory could have been tested out at once. Lying awake in the small hours, she found plenty of flaws in it. She was glad she had resisted the temptation to cheer Wendy up with hints of an alternative solution, for indeed it was a forlorn hope.

Neither had she confided in the family, at least, not fully. Linnaeus knew of her conjecture about the wastepipe, but when he inquired how she had got on with the detective, Lucy only replied that he had seemed interested and had promised to see about it. She said nothing about the plot to impersonate Ivor, or her own intention of breaking the Sabbath, because Linnaeus might disapprove, for one thing, and, for another, he was quite sure to laugh.

Ivor did not come home from Beechfield till nearly midnight. He said there had been no word from Roland, and Wendy was very disappointed and worried.

On Sunday morning the sun again shone out with callous indifference on the dusty gardens of Clonmeen. The heat wave had now reached the stage when everything wants watering and the rainwater tanks are empty, when flowers go over in a day, and fruit rots, and if you pick up a fallen plum it is full of wasps. The gardeners of Clonmeen were reduced to hoping that if nothing else broke the drought, it would rain for the Flower Show.

Lucy counted on getting her family off to church before the plainclothes man turned up to shame her. She made Linnaeus and Ivor start early without her. What they would think when she failed to turn up for the service, she could not imagine. She could only hope that by the time she saw them again she would have an excuse for her divagations.

To her relief it turned out to be an auspicious day. The men went off meekly without arguing, and old Lizzie, for a wonder, showed no curiosity when, five minutes after they had left, there was a man asking for Miss Lucy at the door. The plainclothes man was not as bad as she had feared. Though not in the least like Ivor, he might easily have been one of his friends, except that he was more respectable.

Norah and Theresa, at any rate, took him perfectly for granted when he and Lucy walked into the kitchen at Annalee Hall. Lucy's inclination was to hurry him upstairs out of sight. To her dismay, he engaged in conversation.

"Nuisance when a pipe gets stopped up like that," he remarked to Norah. "I suppose it had been getting choked for some time back."

"No, sir," said Norah, immediately on the defensive. "There wasn't a sign of it getting blocked or I'd have poured some boiling water and soda down it. There was nothing wrong with it that morning, and I doing out the room."

"Is that so? The water was running through all right then? I suppose that would be around nine o'clock?"

Lucy realized that he was checking her story. Luckily Norah showed no surprise at this passion for precision. She had come to take cross questioning as a matter of course.

"Around eleven," she corrected him..

"Do you always do the rooms as late as that?"

Norah not unnaturally looked annoyed. "Her ladyship didn't get up till after breakfast."

"Oh, pardon me. So the water was running through at eleven and two hours later the pipe was stopped. I wonder now, what did it. Well, we'll soon see. Could you lend me a bucket? Thanks. Don't bother to come up."

The plainclothes man viewed the old-fashioned installation in the bedroom and remarked that it was quite an antique. Then he seemed disinclined for further conversation; his affability, Lucy guessed, was only a mask. He got out his tools and set keenly to work. Lucy made herself go and stand over by the window, so as not to annoy him by hovering.

There was silence, except for one expletive from the man at work, when, on his unscrewing the trap underneath the basin, a stream of dirty water shot out, partly into the bucket and partly on to the bedroom carpet. Lucy was watching so intently that she stepped into the puddle without noticing. Along with the water there came a lump of grease and muck, in which were embedded certain fibrous fragments. Lucy felt like Einstein may have, on learning that his theory of relativity was confirmed by astronomical observation.

The plainclothes man took a tin from his pocket and put the whole greasy mess into it, together with more fragments which he had scraped out from inside the pipes. He wrote carefully on a label which was pasted on the lid. Then he stood up and nodded to Lucy.

"Mucky job," he remarked, and bent over the basin to wash his hands. Unfortunately, he had forgotten to screw up the trap again, so another stream of water poured over the carpet. Lucy jumped back and the plainclothes man hastily turned off the tap and put matters right underneath. After this *contretemps* had passed, Lucy at last found words for her mounting excitement.

"Those little chopped up bits!" she exclaimed. "Wouldn't you say they're roots?"

It seemed a new idea to her companion. "I wouldn't know. Is that what you were expecting? Somebody been putting some roots down the drain?"

"He washed the grater!" cried Lucy. "I knew he had to wash it somewhere. The grater that was missing from the kitchen on Sunday morning. And Lord Barna has an alibi."

The plainclothes man did not seem greatly excited. As a matter of fact, he knew little about the case, as he had only been temporarily borrowed from the watch for a man who had been cutting the tails off fox furs unbeknown to their wearers. However, he seemed pleased that Lucy was pleased.

They left the empty bedroom that had given up its secret. On their way through the kitchen the plainclothes man restored the bucket to Norah, and told her he was afraid a drop of water had gone on the floor, which was an understatement. So Norah went up, grumbling, with a cloth, while Theresa, making eyes at the plainclothes man behind Lucy's back, decided that it must have been in the army young Mr. Bex learned to wink like that.

"What next?" asked Lucy, pausing outside in the shrubbery. The plainclothes man informed her that Inspector Lancey himself was waiting at the barracks. He had orders to go straight back, and there was no objection to her coming along.

They found the detective in a little back den of the barracks, something like a housemaid's cupboard, which the Station Sergeant used as his private office. Lucy sat down on his spare chair and left the talking to the plainclothes man. He stood to attention and recited in a professional monotone, while Inspector Lancey scribbled on his papers and avoided his minion's unwinking stare.

The plainclothes man reported that at eleven-thirty that morning, in pursuance of instructions, he had accompanied Miss Bex to Annalee Hall and had examined the toilet fixture in the upstairs front bedroom, formerly jointly occupied by the deceased and her husband, the wastepipe of which was blocked. He had previously ascertained from the housemaid that the said pipe had been blocked at one P.M.. last Sunday, but had not been blocked at eleven A.M.., at which hour the said housemaid did the room. He had extracted from the pipe fragments of fluff, hair, soap and fibrous matter embedded in grease. He had placed specimens in a sealed tin, labeling them with the date and place where found, and had returned immediately to barracks.

"You'd better write that out," said the Inspector. He had a look inside the tin and grunted. "This'll have to go over to Kilmainham for analysis. You could take it over on your bike this afternoon."

The plainclothes man saluted and passed out of Lucy's life.

Left alone with Inspector Lancey, Lucy could not restrain her anxiety. "Are you satisfied about Lord Barna now?" she asked.

But the Inspector shook his head. "He hasn't given us much of an answer to those questions we wanted to ask him. About that book, for instance. He says he never touched it, fingerprints or no fingerprints. Where's the sense of talking like that?"

"But this fresh evidence"—she pointed to the tin of specimens—

"seeing what you know about the times, isn't it in his favor?"

"Now, Miss Bex, in our work it doesn't do to jump to conclusions. We've got to wait for the analyst's report, for one thing."

Lucy sighed. No use hoping for a policeman to be anything but non-committal. She said,

"I'd like to have sent a message to his fiancée, Miss Nichol-Jervis."

"Better not. At this stage the less said the better. It isn't only him we've got to think about. If we let him go too soon, we might spoil our chance of making another arrest."

That sounded more encouraging, Lucy thought.

"Then you'll act on the report from Kilmainham?"

"If it's what we think."

"And if the roots are *Aconitum ferox,* you'll release Lord Barna?"

The Inspector did not promise. "If the roots are *Aconitum ferox,*" he said grimly, "we'll arrest Osmund."

Naturally, Lucy came out of the barracks just in time to join the procession of the faithful coming out of church. But it was no use pretending to have been one of them, not with accurate pew reckoners like the good Protestants of Clonmeen. There was nothing to be done but speed past the Miss Cuffes with a bright, brazen smile, cut the two Mrs. Tallons, drop one's eyes before the shocked expression of Miss Milfoyle, and evade an ironic glance from Miss FitzEustace. Ivor and Linnaeus had to be faced at last, and they were walking, as usual, with Mr. and Mrs. Nichol-Jervis. How Lucy wished she might have given the news of Roland's release! But she dared do no more than inquire sympathetically for Wendy, and then taxed all her powers to put up a smoke screen of small talk.

Her family had the sense to keep from questions till they were alone, but then they had to have the whole story. They all agreed that things did look more hopeful for Roland, but somehow none of them managed to feel very cheerful.

"If they let him out," said Ivor, doing his best, "he'll owe it to Aunt Lucy."

"If they arrest Osmund," said Linnaeus, "he also will owe it to her."

"Don't!" begged Lucy. "I wish I hadn't had anything to do with it. But it was him or Roland."

"Anyhow, Wendy will be pleased," said Ivor, and stamped hard on a snail that he saw crawling across the path.

CHAPTER XXII
A Slip-up

AFTER LUNCH IVOR sloped off again to Beechfield. They did not expect to see him again till bedtime, but he was back at quarter-past six.

"Roland's out," he announced.

It was the Inspector who had himself telephoned to Wendy, to say that Lord Barna was being released on condition that he did not communicate with anybody in Clonmeen. He was to stay in his flat, but Wendy could go in and see him there. Wendy was off at the word.

"I told her it wasn't worth it," said Ivor. "She'd only have half an hour before she had to get the last bus back. But she would go."

"Of course it was worth it," said Lucy. "How kind that was of the Inspector! I always knew he was really human underneath."

Her nephew did not answer; at the moment he was taking a poor view of humans. He turned from them to Remus, the cat. But cats divide people into two classes: those who know when stroking is required of them, and those who insist on stroking to please themselves. Remus transferred Ivor from the first class to the second and haughtily removed himself. So Ivor went and fiddled with the wireless, till sounds of one station after another in quick succession if not together exasperated Lucy into finding him something useful to do. Inventing jobs for him, and standing over him while he did them, kept her from giving a thought to Mr. Osmund or Lord Barna for the rest of the evening.

Dullness drove the Bexes to bed early, but the day was not over yet. At eleven there came a knock at the door. Linnaeus went down in his dressing gown to answer it.

"No," Lucy heard him say. "No, we haven't had anybody here. Certainly come in and look round. Just a minute and I'll get you the garden keys."

There was a trampling of men through the hall. Linnaeus called from under Lucy's bedroom window. She looked out over the garden and saw a large dark mass of Civic Guard detach itself from the shadows by the honeysuckle trellis and hurtle over the grass. Somebody else was opening and shutting doors in the yard.

"Throw me down my tennis shoes, would you?" said Linnaeus. "You'll find them in the heap under the washstand."

"What's up, Father?" asked Ivor out of his own window farther along.

"The police are looking for Osmund," said Linnaeus. "They went to arrest him just now, and he made a bolt for it."

Ivor let himself down from the window sill and dropped beside Linnaeus. Lucy found the tennis shoes, and then went to calm old Lizzie. There was another knock at the door; answering it herself, she found Inspector Lancey.

Lucy received the Inspector as an old friend, but he looked at her severely.

"May I come in, Miss Bex, for a short time?"

"Oh yes, do, Inspector," said Lucy, "but do you mind waiting till I put some things on?" She felt she could meet any emergency better with her hair up. She also told old Lizzie to get the kitchen fire going again and put a kettle on, because it is always useful in emergencies to have a kettle boiling and it would keep Lizzie quiet. Then she rejoined the Inspector in the garden room.

"Will you have a bottle of beer, Inspector?" she asked him hospitably. The Inspector said he never touched anything while on duty, and she felt crushed.

The Inspector mentioned that he had sent a Guard to find Linnaeus and Ivor, because he had something he wanted to say to all of them. Till they came he stood by the window and brooded. Lucy sat down and began to knit. Linnaeus had gone along, not so much to help the search party search as to keep it off the flower beds. In this he had not succeeded very well. He and Ivor came in together, both looking cross.

The Bexes dropped automatically into their usual chairs. The Inspector preferred to keep standing.

"You know what's happened?" he asked abruptly.

"You tell us," said Ivor. "All we know is that Osmund slipped you."

"Oh, is that all? Have I your word for that?"

"Look here, Inspector," said Linnaeus, "what are you getting at?"

The Inspector looked from one to the other of them.

"You don't know where he is? You wouldn't by any chance be helping him to evade arrest?"

"My God!" said Ivor. "Considering that but for Aunt Lucy you'd never have known—"

"I'm not forgetting what we owe Miss Bex," the Inspector' interrupted him. "Isn't it just because of that I've come?" He looked at Lucy. "I don't know how far your assistance was what I'd call disinterested. Weren't you acting more to get his lordship out of jail than to get anyone else in? It seemed to me you might not care about being responsible for the arrest of Osmund, and that might induce you to lend a hand in his escape."

"How clever of you, Inspector!" said Lucy, forgetting to be annoyed because she was struck by his psychological insight. "But I assure you, I know nothing about it."

"Aunt Lucy isn't like that," Ivor informed him. "She's always on the side of law and order."

"Then there aren't many like her," stated the Inspector. "Not in this country."

"Oh, we're very Anglo," said Ivor.

"Yes. I could see that."

Although the Inspector's tone had become more conciliatory, the Bexes felt he was still cross with them and the injustice rankled. The truth was, he was angry with himself, and he transferred some of it to them, his own men having already had their share. It was maddening that the arrest should have been bungled.

An interruption at this point was opportune. It came from old Lizzie, who poked a wild and wispy head round the door, to say the kettle was boiling, and did Miss Lucy want tea? Miss Lucy thought tea would be a good idea. She was a little nervous of offering it to the Inspector, in view of his earlier attitude, but when she said, "Four cups, Lizzie," he made no objection, so she hoped he was softening.

When the door had shut again the Inspector said,

"I'd like to tell you what we know now about your man Osmund. It's right you should all know what sort of a man you had for a neighbor over there.

"Miss Bex'll have told you about the evidence we had against Lord Barna. That book, now, with his fingerprints all over it. There was something funny about those prints. As I might say, something phony. They were all over the cover, in quite a natural position for holding a book, but what wasn't natural was that we couldn't find any more on the inside pages. This cover, mind you, wasn't the actual cover of the book itself, it was a brown paper one that anybody could put on. So we asked his lordship if he had any other books in brown paper covers, and he said he usually put them on his textbooks, when he remembered, the ones he was reading for exams. He'd be selling them again when the exams were over and it paid to keep them clean. He made out a rough list, and we had a look round his flat and his office. There was one book, *Spicer and Pegler on Auditing*, that he said had a cover on and it hadn't. You see? It was just the same size as this other book *Poisonous Plants,* and the cover off *Poisonous Plants* fitted it perfectly. See what your man had done? Switched the cover from one book to the other, to throw suspicion on somebody else."

"Smart work!" grinned Ivor.

"Ivor!" said Lucy, shocked.

"Ingenious," said Linnaeus, "but it would have been safer just to get rid of the book."

"That might have drawn attention to it," said the Inspector. "Once we start looking round, it's not so easy to discard or destroy anything without our noticing. He should have thought of it long before, but he counted on the crime passing as an accident. When he saw us still nosing round after the inquest, he got the wind up and tried to incriminate the other fellow.

"And yet, as it turned out, he really did him a good turn. We thought for some time that they might have been collaborating. But Osmund wasn't so clever as he thought he was when he put that bit of monkshood root in the turn-ups of the other fellow's trousers.

"With all his ideas about fingerprints, it never occurred to him that that was where he'd left his own. When you grate anything up you're apt to be left with a last lump over that's too short to rub through. Well, that was how Osmund had this end bit of root, with a beautiful clear print of his own thumb."

"What!" said Lucy. "Why, I suppose you knew all about that on Saturday. You might have told me. You didn't really need me to bring you any evidence at all."

"You can't have too much evidence," said the Inspector. "What you gave us strengthened our case. I don't say we were certain by Saturday what had happened, but we were getting there all right. Slow but sure, you know. It's all routine."

The phrase "machinery of the law" might have been coined to fit Inspector Lancey. He was so methodical and impersonal in his investigations. As he talked he had been observing the reactions of the Bexes, still hoping to find some clue to the escaped man's whereabouts. Whether or not he was satisfied of their innocence, he had talked himself into a better humor and said kindly to Lucy, "That bit of root you brought in to me, Miss Bex, was nothing worse than a dandelion. But you made a good guess about the wastepipe. The fingerprint evidence alone mightn't be enough for a jury. So you see, every little bit helps." And that, Lucy realized, was all the acknowledgment she could expect.

"There's another thing that'll come out at the trial," the Inspector went on, "that ought to remove any doubts the jury have left. D'you remember the evidence at the inquest about the phone calls? Remember how Osmund was supposed to have rung up three different doctors and they were all away? Then in the end, it was his lordship who put a call through.

"We tried to trace those first calls, and we didn't succeed. The only genuine phone call made from Annalee Hall that afternoon was the one Lord Barna put through to Dr. Brett. The other calls weren't recorded at all. Osmund must have been only pretending to phone, probably played the old trick of dialing his own number every time. Lord Barna was watching, but he wouldn't be acute enough to notice that. And the man's wife was dying upstairs."

"Good God!" said Linnaeus. "How absolutely cold-blooded."

"That's your murderer," said the Inspector. "I've been telling you all this so that you won't be too much carried away by sympathy for the hunted man."

Lucy was looking rather sick. "Thank you, Inspector, you have convinced me."

"But from your point of view," said Ivor, "I'm afraid you've wasted your time. He isn't here and never was."

"Then it beats all where he can have got to."

Tea had arrived by this time, as Lucy knew from a sound of bumping in the hall. Old Lizzie could not bring the tray in, because that would have involved appearing before the gentlemen in her night attire, so she put it down on the floor outside, put her head in as before, and said "Tea's ready" and disappeared. Ivor now fetched the things in, and it was a welcome refreshment for their spirits.

Once more they ventured to ask the Inspector what had happened about Mr. Osmund. He did not like telling the story. It all came of sending two less experienced officers to Annalee Hall instead of going himself.

Between them, the subordinates had made a fine hash of it.

"I told them to be civil," said the Inspector bitterly. "I never expected them to be such eejuts. They were late getting there, to begin with. We were all held up waiting for those fellows at Kilmainham to come through with that report, and then it took time to get the warrant, and on top of all, going out there in a police car they had a puncture and had to stop and change a wheel. So they didn't arrive at the house till around half-past ten, and everybody had already gone to bed. When they knocked, Osmund himself came to an upstairs window and asked what they wanted, and they said they'd like to speak to him a minute, and he told them to wait there and he'd come down. Well, they waited there like a couple of fools for near on five minutes, and nothing happened, and they knocked again and nothing happened. And then at last they knocked the maids up and got in, but by that time, of course, your man Osmund was well away. He'd gone out by the back door and through the yard, and beyond that, not a sign of him."

"What, no footprints?" asked Ivor.

"Too many footprints," said the Inspector. "Especially after my two great gobdaws had been playing hide-and-go-seek in the dark. They wasted a good ten minutes looking for him themselves before they phoned me at the barracks. But we've men on all the roads now, and I'd say he couldn't get far."

"So you think he must be hiding somewhere?"

"He hadn't time to get far along the road," answered the Inspector. "He'd no bicycle, and our cordon was out before eleven. He might slip by one man in the dark with luck, but he wouldn't get far. But we've combed the grounds of the Hall and Annalee House as well as here, and so far there isn't a smell of him."

"I wouldn't expect him to be over at the McGoldricks'," said Lucy. "They hardly knew each other, if that, and I'm sure he wasn't familiar with the lie of the land."

"Well, I was betting on his being here," said the Inspector, "but it seems I guessed wrong. Ah well, he may get a little way in the dark, but once daylight comes, I'd say he'd be easy cot. I'm sorry now to have disturbed you and kept you up so late."

He shook hands with them, which they took to mean they were forgiven. Then the Inspector departed to visit his men on the watch. A good many Civic Guards were in for a sleepless night, and the Bexes themselves slept poorly after the tea and the excitement and were conscious of trampling and muttering outside long after they had finally gone to bed.

CHAPTER XXIII
Double Arrest

NEXT MORNING FOUND the Guards still at it. Ivor went out before breakfast and learned that there was still no sign of the escaped man. They
were stopping all vehicles along the road and had suffered some scath-
ing criticism from Mr. McGoldrick, who was starting early for Drogheda
with his van full of samples. Lucy thought of sending some coffee to the
nearest outpost, but Linnaeus, who had been out early, reported that the
strawberry runners he had been pegging in over the weekend had all
been trampled, and he was almost sure about two dozen greengages had
gone from the tree on the wall, so she did not dare.

However, keeping in touch with the search party gave Ivor something to do, and when she had got Linnaeus off to town and done the
beds and the orders and the laundry, which went on Mondays, Lucy
thought she would at last have a chance to bottle the tomatoes, which
was getting urgent. She had picked seven or eight pounds of them when
Wendy Nichol-Jervis appeared.

They sat under the apple tree again. Lucy thought, "When I've done
the tomatoes, I must pick up windfalls for jelly," and half her mind went
off on calculations regarding sugar and space on the kitchen stove. Wendy
handed her a note from Roland.

> "DEAR MISS BEX,
> Thank you for saving my neck. Your kindness has been the
> one ray of light.
>
> > Yours, undeserving,
> > ROLAND."

"He hadn't time for more," Wendy explained, "because I had
to catch the bus. But he hopes to come and see you as soon as he can
get away."

Lucy privately hoped that she would not have any more visitors till
she had got her tomatoes done, and the Morello cherries, which were
overdue for bottling as well. The hot weather had ripened everything up

just in the very week when she had no time to attend to them. Two rows of peas had come in together instead of in succession and were going to waste because she could not pick them fast enough, and she dared not even look at the French beans. It was ridiculous to start sidelines like amateur detection when you had a garden on your hands.

Wendy, eyeing the baskets of tomatoes, offered help, and Lucy accepted it, which was a compliment. Wendy was a person who could be made to understand how you wanted a thing done, and who could be trusted to put the ripest fruit, of which there was a great deal, into a separate basket for pulping, the firmer, yellow-red, tomatoes being kept for bottling. Far too many assistants would get talking and forget about the distinction, or else would keep bothering you to decide about borderline cases. Wendy could even be admitted into the kitchen without disorganizing old Lizzie. She was a sterling girl, and it was nonsense for Roland to talk about "the one ray of light" when he had been so lucky in his fiancée.

They carried out a tray of jars and cut up and packed the tomatoes under the apple tree. It was a pleasant place on such a lovely morning.

"Women are lucky, on the whole," Wendy remarked, "to have jobs like this to take their minds off things."

Lucy glanced at her sympathetically and thought she had not quite recovered from the strain of the last few days. It was hard to believe that the duration of the mystery, from the day of the murder to the issuing of a warrant for the arrest of Mr. Osmund, was only one week. In dangerous situations, impressions of one's surroundings become distorted, so that trees, cliffs, buildings, seem much larger than they really are. In the same way, the period when they were all groping in a fog of suspicion seemed to have lasted for weeks. But the air had cleared now.

Ought she to hope that, after all, the police would never succeed in bringing Mr. Osmund to justice? There was a kind of horror, all the same, in the thought of his existence. The murder had been so cruel and so systematic, and varnished over afterwards with such hypocrisy. How does a human being turn into a monster?

She could not help saying something of what she thought to Wendy.

"Roland says it was money," replied Wendy, and her voice sounded shocked and incredulous. The Nichol-Jervises had inherited a comfortable income and the sense to manage it comfortably. Wendy would no more have wasted money than the garden water supply, but she was used to having it on tap. So she looked puzzled as she told Lucy, "I believe they had quite a lot of rows about Lady Madeleine's extravagance. Giving up their house in town and coming here was meant to be an economy, but Lady Madeleine kept on going up to stay in hotels and shop, and she had the house done up, and she was planning to spend a whole lot more on the garden. Mr. Osmund didn't seem able to stop her, somehow."

"Couldn't he afford it then?"

"Roland says Mr. Osmund said they had never lived within their income since they were married, but whatever he said to Lady Madeleine, she only made a joke of it. But if it was as serious as all that, surely there would be some legal way of making her keep to an allowance?"

"Of course there would," said Lucy. "But once they had begun to quarrel—" she sighed. "And yet, when you met them they seemed to be getting on all right."

"I don't know about that," said Wendy thoughtfully. "She never took much notice of him, did she? He just used to smoulder in the background."

"She had a very dominating personality."

"Roland was fond of her. But then, she was all the family he had since his grandfather died. She spoiled him. She used to flirt with his tutors and give him enormous tips. And when he left school she liked him to go about with her, even after she was married. She just couldn't have too many men around." Wendy's voice was unwontedly acid. "I can't help it, Lucy, I do think she was a silly woman."

Lucy sighed again. "No sillier than some. But a type we don't get much in Clonmeen. Here's Ivor back again."

Ivor came striding through the French windows, looking as if he brought news.

"Wendy!" he exclaimed. "Nobody told me you were coming. Listen! Osmund's been taken at last."

"Alive?" cried Lucy. Ivor nodded. She had been certain that he would have committed suicide.

"Where?" asked Wendy.

"Five miles this side of Drogheda."

"Of *Drogheda?* How on earth could he get to Drogheda?"

"In Mr. McGoldrick's van."

It was asking too much of them to believe this until Ivor had told the whole story. Extraordinary as this was, it did become just credible if you knew Mr. McGoldrick.

It will be remembered that Mr. McGoldrick and Mr. Osmund had never met, but that, though the former did not know the latter at all, Osmund knew what Mr. McGoldrick looked like, and quite a lot of other things about him, from the conversation of the night he had dined at the Bexes'. He knew, for instance, that he was in the habit of leaving Clonmeen by car every Monday morning.

On Sunday night when the police arrived, Osmund escaped from the house in too much of a hurry to have any clear idea where he was going, and then he saw a light in Mr. McGoldrick's study window. Mr. McGoldrick was sitting up alone, after the rest of the family had gone to bed, finishing *Bull Dog Drummond.* Osmund went and tapped at the window, and, inspired perhaps by seeing what Mr. McGoldrick was reading, he spun him a complicated tale. He said he was a British secret service man sent over to keep a watch on the German Legation, and that it was through their machinations that the police were on his track. He was in danger of being arrested on a trumped-up charge, and although he could easily clear himself it would end in his being interned, whereas it was essential that he should get back to England with certain information.

Even as they talked, the police came to the front door. They foolishly did not explain what the excitement was about, or even mention Osmund by name. They simply asked if the McGoldricks had seen "a man." Mr. McGoldrick thrilled at the chance of doing something for England. He hid Osmund under the study table till the police had gone and afterwards made him comfortable in the garage for the night. Next morning they made a hiding place in the van behind the sample boxes. The Civic Guard who looked into the van, like those who came to the house, was perfunctory in his inspection. After all, everybody knew old McGoldrick, and he was the last man anybody would have suspected of sheltering a murderer.

They got well away along the Drogheda road. Osmund's idea was to get across to England on some cargo boat and pose as someone who had lost everything in the blitz. But the luck he had had up to then deserted him. The charcoal engine broke down, as it so often had before. The attention of the Guards was drawn to them. By this time Osmund's description had been circulated, the registration number of the car showed that it came from the Clonmeen area, and that was enough to get the two of them arrested.

So the Guards at Clonmeen were taken off the roads. Sergeant

Dunphy thankfully said good-bye to Inspector Lancey and was able to give his mind to filling up forms again. Lucy never saw the Inspector again except at the trial, when they exchanged the briefest civilities.

Everybody in Clonmeen was sorry for Mr. McGoldrick. It was felt that he had acted, though foolishly, from creditable motives, and he even became something of a hero. His van was confiscated and he was sent to prison for six months, but was not too uncomfortable there. So many leading public men in Ireland have served prison sentences that prison reform has received more attention than some other social measures, nor does a jail record carry quite the social stigma that it may elsewhere.

Otway Osmund was convicted and hanged. It was a less painful death than he had chosen for his victim, but the preceding period of suspense and anticipation may be thought to have balanced the account.

CHAPTER XXIV
The Flower Show

THE REST OF THE WEEK sped on wings of preparation for the Flower Show. It was the very best thing to help everybody to forget the murder. At Annalee Lodge, they talked of nothing but where to have the tea if it rained, how to get the vases out from Dublin, when the marquee would arrive, who was to receive Mr. O'Gallchobhair, and what the band would drink.

Linnaeus prowled about tying bits of colored wool round the stems of things he thought he might want to exhibit. Ivor ran errands, many of which seemed to take him through Beechfield. Lucy made plans and then remade them to suit other people's arrangements. Exhibits were to be in the marquee in the paddock, with the band on a platform adjoining; tea would be on the lawn under the apple tree; unless it rained there would be no need to have people in the house. But then Miss FitzEustace came and offered to hold a show of flower paintings, and the only place for that seemed to be the dining-room, and that meant a stand up buffet lunch, as pictures would be occupying all the chairs. The garden room was to be sacred to the entertainment of Mr. O'Gallchobhair. If it rained, they would clear the coach house and have tea partly there and partly in the kitchen. In that case, Lucy's bedroom would be her one remaining refuge.

The weather changed into the worst kind for organizing anything: the whole sky underhung with stuffy clouds and the pressure of the atmosphere making itself felt. Thunder was once heard rumbling in the distance, but it held off, and on Saturday morning, once Linnaeus and Ivor had finished moving a ton of wood blocks from the coach house, and old Lizzie had arranged laurel branches to hide the untidiest corners of the kitchen, the sun shone out and blandly assured them of its patronage for the day.

The first eager exhibitors arrived before the Bexes had finished breakfast and much earlier than the stewards appointed by the Committee to look after them. When the stewards did come they were kept busy. By the middle of the morning the marquee was crowded, and the noise and excitement were equal to a bargain sale in a parrot house.

Somehow everybody was provided with a vase and water to put in it. Ambiguities in the Schedule were cleared up; "Vase of Roses (one bloom of any variety)" was held to mean as many different roses as the McGoldricks' gardener wanted to put in and not one bloom only, as it was interpreted by Christina Duffy. Unpleasantness was narrowly averted when Mrs. Tallon was permitted to transfer her entry of phloxes from a class for Annuals to one for Hardy Cut Flowers. Miss Lottie Cuffe was appeased when someone upset a vase of water over her entry of soda bread. Lucy kept out of all this, being fully occupied in keeping the peace between old Lizzie and the tea helpers, but Linnaeus was in the thick of it and kept being called in to give delicate decisions, while he hunted up and down the tent for his own certain winners in the pea class, which had been cooked, by mistake, for dinner the night before.

Toward half-past twelve, the last exhibitors were shepherded out of the marquee, and the judges were ceremoniously ushered in. They did their duty so conscientiously that they could not be persuaded in to lunch till nearly two. What with judges and helpers, about thirty people crowded into the dining-room for soup and sandwiches. They had a private preview of Miss FitzEustace's pictures, and one of the judges bought one before the show opened at all.

Then Lucy madly changed her frock, in company with three helpers who had turned up with suitcases, saying they knew she wouldn't mind if they popped up to her bedroom. When she came down the crowd had thickened, the band had arrived, and Mr. O'Gallchobhair was in the middle of his speech. She listened respectfully to the end of it, which was in Irish, stood pointedly to attention while the band rendered *The Soldier's Song* and then, as Linnaeus and the distinguished visitor moved off, to waltz time, to inspect the exhibits, she turned with relief to Mrs. Nichol-Jervis.

"You look worn out," Mrs. Nichol-Jervis told her inconsiderately. "Do come and have a quiet cup of tea."

Lucy pointed out that it was only half-past three, but Mrs. Nichol-Jervis said it was essential to get in before the rush. They sat down under the apple tree where Roland had confided his troubles to Lucy and Wendy had wept in Ivor's arms. For the first time in several days, Lucy's thoughts returned to the tragedy.

She asked how Roland was. He had been staying a day or two at Beechfield, while attending to the closing of Annalee Hall. Mrs. Nichol-Jervis replied,

"We think he has taken it all very well. One had not expected him, somehow, to show much character, but although there is not much he can actively do, he is very quiet and sensible. We feel very sorry for him. Ernest is trying to interest him in the garden, and only yesterday he mowed all the grass in the front with the small hand mower."

"I am so glad," said Lucy approvingly. "I always knew you would like him when you once got to know him."

"Yes, we do," said Mrs. Nichol-Jervis. "I must say, it is easier to like him now we haven't got to regard him as one of the family."

"But haven't you?"

Mrs. Nichol-Jervis looked surprised. "Why no, not now. Do you mean to say you haven't been told? I took it for granted you would have been the first to know."

"Are you telling me they have broken it off?"

"Of course they have."

"But I thought " Lucy was bewildered. "Wendy seemed so upset when he was arrested."

"Naturally," said Wendy's mother. "Wendy is so tenderhearted. But what made it worse for her was, that she had decided even then that they were not really suited, and she simply had not the heart to tell him so, under the circumstances. So you see, she was in a wretchedly false position, and it might have gone on for months, if it had not been for you."

"Poor Roland!" said Lucy.

"Oh, he'll get over it," said Mrs. Nichol-Jervis easily. "It was obvious from the first that it could never come to anything. It's a great relief to have it all settled without embarrassment. Now they are the best of friends, and he talks of going on the stage."

Lucy meditated. The stage, she thought, was quite a good place for Lord Barna. It was another aspect of the situation that caused her a foolish twinge at the heart.

"Have you seen Ivor anywhere?" she asked.

Mrs. Nichol-Jervis smiled. "I saw him during *The Soldier's Song,*" she said, "kissing my daughter behind the honeysuckle trellis. I always say it's hard to get *Lonicera* to thicken into a really satisfactory screen."

THE END

Rue Morgue Press Titles as of Januaray 2001

Brief Candles by Manning Coles. From Topper to Aunt Dimity, mystery readers have embraced the cozy ghost story. Four of the best were written by Manning Coles, the creator of the witty Tommy Hambledon spy novels. First published in 1954, *Brief Candles* is likely to produce more laughs than chills as a young couple vacationing in France run into two gentlemen with decidedly old-world manners. What they don't know is that James and Charles Latimer are ancestors of theirs who shuffled off this mortal coil some 80 years earlier when, emboldened by strong drink and with only a pet monkey and an aged waiter as allies, the two made a valiant, foolish and quite fatal attempt to halt a German advance during the Franco-Prussian War of 1870. Now these two ectoplasmic gentlemen and their spectral pet monkey Ulysses have been summoned from their unmarked graves because their visiting relatives are in serious trouble. But before they can solve the younger Latimers' problems, the three benevolent spirits light brief candles of insanity for a tipsy policeman, a recalcitrant banker, a convocation of English ghostbusters, and a card-playing rogue who's wanted for murder."For those who like something out of the ordinary. Lighthearted, very funny.'—*The Sunday Times*. **0-915230-24-0 $14.00. Happy Returns (0-915230-31-3, $14.00)** and **Come and Go (0915230-34-8, $14.00)** complete the trilogy. Equally funny is a stand-alone ghost story, **The Far Traveller (0-915230-35-6, $14.00)** set in a German castle.

The Chinese Chop by Juanita Sheridan. "The reprint of (this) 1949 novel, besides offering a well-written and enjoyable variant of the boarding-housse whodunit and a vivid picture of the post WWII New York City housing shortage, puts the lie to the common misconception that strong, self-reliant, non-spinster-or-comic female sleuths didn't appear on the scene until the 1970s. Chinese-American Lily Wu and her novelist Watson, janice Cameron, are young and feminine but not dependent on men, and it's hard to imagine how even Asian-American readers could object to the admirable Ily, some now-politically-incorrect terminolgy apart. According to Tom & Enid's Schantz's typically informative introduction, Rue Morgue will also reprint the subsequent three books in a regrettably short series."—Jon L. Breen, *Ellery Queen's Mystery Magazine*. Anthony Boucher (for whom Bouchercon, the World Mystery Convention, is named) described Lily as "the exquisitely blended product of Eastern and Western cultures" and the only female sleuth that he "was devotedly in love with," citing "that odd mixture of respect for her professional skills and delight in her personal charms."   **0-915230-32-1 $14.00**

Death on Milestone Buttress by Glyn Carr. Abercrombie ("Filthy") Lewker was looking forward to a fortnight of climbing in Wales after a grueling season touring England with his Shakespearean company. Young Hilary Bourne thought the fresh air would be a pleasant change from her dreary job at the bank, as well as a chance to renew her acquaintance with a certain young scientist. Neither one expected this bucolic outing to turn deadly but when one of their party is killed in an apparent accident during what should have been an easy climb on the Milestone Buttress, Filthy and Hilary turn detective. Nearly everyone had reason to hate the victim but each had an alibi for the time of the murder. "You'll get a taste of the Welsh countryside, will encounter names replete with consonants, will be exposed to numerous snippets from Shakespeare and will find Carr's novel a worthy representative of the cozies of two generations ago."–John A. Broussard, *I Love a Mystery*.   **0-915230-29-1 $14.00**

Black Corridors by Constance & Gwenyth Little. Jessie Warren's Aunt Isabel checked herself into a hospital to enjoy a spot of imagined ill-health.That's about the time someone decided to start killing blondes. For the first time in her life Jessie's glad to have her bright red hair, even if a certain doctor—who doesn't have the money or the looks of her other beaux—enjoys making fun of those flaming locks. After Jessie stumbles across a couple of bodies and starts snooping around, the murderer decides to switch from blondes to redheads in this 1940 charmer.   **0-915230-33-X**   **$14.00**

The Black Stocking by Constance & Gwenyth Little. Irene Hastings, who can't decide which of her two fiancés she should marry, is looking forward to a nice vacation, and everything would have been just fine had not her mousy friend Ann asked to be dropped off at an insane asylum so she could visit her sister. When the sister escapes, just about everyone, including a handsome young doctor, mistakes Irene for the runaway loony, and she is put up at an isolated private hospital under house arrest, pending final identification. First published in 1946. "Wacky....witty....madcap....highly recommended."—D.L. Browne, *I Love a Mystery.*   **0-915230-30-5**   **$14.00**

The Black-Headed Pins by Constance & Gwenyth Little. "...a zany, fun-loving puzzler spun by the sisters Little—it's celluloid screwball comedy printed on paper. The charm of this book lies in the lively banter between characters and the breakneck pace of the story."—Diane Plumley, *Dastardly Deeds.* "For a strong example of their work, try (this) very funny and inventive 1938 novel of a dysfunctional family Christmas." Jon L. Breen, *Ellery Queen's Mystery Magazine.*   **0-915230-25-9**   **$14.00**

The Black Gloves by Constance & Gwenyth Little. "I'm relishing every madcap moment."—*Murder Most Cozy.*   **0-915230-20-8**   **$14.00**

The Black Honeymoon by Constance & Gwenyth Little. Can you murder someone with feathers? If you don't believe feathers are lethal, then you probably haven't read a Little mystery. No, Uncle Richard wasn't tickled to death—though we can't make the same guarantee for readers—but the hyper-allergic rich man did manage to sneeze himself into the hereafter. First published in 1944. Picked by Deadly Passions as onf the ten best presented mysteries of the year.   **0-915230-21-6 $14.00**

Great Black Kanba by Constance & Gwenyth Little. "If you love train mysteries as much as I do, hop on the Trans-Australia Railway in *Great Black Kanba*, a fast and funny 1944 novel by the talented (Littles)."—Jon L. Breen, *Ellery Queen's Mystery Magazine.* "I have decided to add *Kanba* to my favorite mysteries of all time list!...a zany ride I'll definitely take again and again."—Diane Plumley in the Murder Ink newsletter.   **0-915230-22-4 $14.00**

The Grey Mist Murders by Constance & Gwenyth Little. Who—or what—is the mysterious figure that emerges from the grey mist to strike down several passengers on the final leg of a round-the-world sea voyage? This 1938 effort was the Littles' first book.   **0-915230-26-7 $14.00**

The Black Paw by Constance & Gwenyth Little. From the 1941 dustjacket copy: Callie Drake, charming, bat-brained, and trouble attracting, undertook to assist a friend and was immediately involved in a first-class mess. Callie had intended to some highly justifiable petty larceny, but the police figured that murder was the motive for her appearance in the Barton household masquerading as a housemaid. It was true that Callie was the last person to have seen George, whose religious visions kept him up late at night, and it was Callie's room in which Frannie Barton met her death. Callie saw the isolated print of an animal's paw, and Callie saw the rocking chair swaying when no one was in the room.   **0-915230-37-2 $14.00**

Murder is a Collector's Item by Elizabeth Dean. "(It) froths over with the same effervescent humor as the best Hepburn-Grant films."—Sujata Massey. "Completely enjoyable."—*New York Times.* "Fast and funny."—*The New Yorker.* Twenty-six-year-old Emma Marsh isn't much at spelling or geography and perhaps she butchers the odd literary quotation or two, but she's a keen judge of character and more than able to hold her own when it comes to selling antiques or solving murders. . Smoothly written and sparkling with dry, sophisticated humor, this milestone combines an intriguing puzzle with an entertaining portrait of a self-possessed young woman on her own at the end of the Great Depression. **0-915230-19-4 $14.00. Murder is a Serious Business (0-915230-28-3, $14.95)** continues Emma's adventures. "Judging from (this book) it's too bad she didn't write a few more."—Mary Ann Steel, *I Love a Mystery*.

Murder, Chop Chop by James Norman. "The book has the butter-wouldn't-melt-in-his-mouth cool of Rick in *Casablanca*."—*The Rocky Mountain News*. "Amuses the reader no end."—*Mystery News*. "This long out-of-print masterpiece is intricately plotted, full of eccentric characters and very humorous indeed. Highly recommended."— *Mysteries by Mail*. Meet Gimiendo Hernandez Quinto, a gigantic Mexican who once rode with Pancho Villa and who now trains *guerrilleros* for the Nationalist Chinese government when he isn't solving murders.   **0-915230-16-X $13.00**

Death at The Dog by Joanna Cannan. "Worthy of being discussed in the same breath with an Agatha Christie or Josephine Tey...anyone who enjoys Golden Age mysteries will surely enjoy this one."—Sally Fellows, *Mystery News*. "Skilled writing and brilliant characterization."—*Times of London*. . Set in late 1939 during the first anxious months of World War II, *Death at The Dog*, which was first published in 1941, is a wonderful example of the classic English detective novel that first flourished between the two World Wars. **0-915230-23-2 $14.00**. The first book in this series is **They Rang Up the Police (0-915230-27-5, $14.00)**. "Just delightful."—*Sleuth of Baker Street* Pick-of-the-Month. "A brilliantly plotted mystery...splendid character study...don't miss this one, folks. It's a keeper."—Sally Fellows, *Mystery News*. Murder in an English village in 1937.   **0-915230-27-5 $14.00**

Cook Up a Crime by Charlotte Murray Russell. "Perhaps the mother of today's 'cozy' mystery . . . amateur sleuth Jane has a personality guaranteed to entertain the most demanding reader."—Andy Plonka, *The Mystery Reader*. "Some wonderful old time recipes...highly recommended."—*Mysteries by Mail*. Meet Jane Amanda Edwards, a self-styled "full-fashioned" spinster who goes looking for recipes and finds a body instead in this 1951 charmer.   **0-915230-18-6 $13.00**

The Man from Tibet by Clyde B. Clason. Locked inside the Tibetan Room of his Chicago luxury apartment, the rich antiquarian was overheard repeating a forbidden occult chant under the watchful eyes of Buddhist gods. When the doors were opened it appeared that he had succumbed to a heart attack. But the elderly Roman historian and sometime amateur sleuth Theocritus Lucius Westborough is convinced that Adam Merriweather's death was anything but natural and that the weapon was an eighth century Tibetan manuscript.   **0-915230-17-8 $14.00**

The Mirror by Marlys Millhiser. "Completely enjoyable."—*Library Journal*. "A great deal of fun."—*Publishers Weekly*. How could you not be intrigued, as one reviewer pointed out, by a novel in which "you find the main character marrying her own grandfather and giving birth to her own mother?" Such is the situation in Marlys Millhiser's classic novel of two women who end up living each other's lives after they look into an antique Chinese mirror.   **0-915230-15-1 $14.95**

About The Rue Morgue Press

The Rue Morgue Press vintage mystery line is designed to bring back into print those books that were favorites of readers between the turn of the century and the 1960s. The editors welcome suggestions for reprints. To receive our catalog or make suggestions, write The Rue Morgue Press, P.O. Box 4119, Boulder, Colorado 80306. (1-800-699-6214).